Forbidden Lessons

"I've been fighting this for so long."

A muscle twitched as he clenched his jaw. He was looking at her, serious, no joy in his expression. His eyes seemed almost sad.

Her stomach was lurching. It was the moment she had longed for, dreamed about, and yet it felt more like a terrible taboo than ecstasy.

He stroked his hand down the side of her face, brushing her hair back.

"This is something that could ruin both our lives," he said.

She couldn't speak. She wanted to tell him that she didn't care, that she only wanted to live for the moment. But she was terrified.

"Wanting you this much… it makes me willing to risk everything."

Tempting Her Teacher

"Being this close to you is like torture. But it's wrong - I'm your teacher."

Catholic school teacher Carl Spencer faces a crisis of faith when he falls for his student Juliet, how can he resist the temptation to be with her?

Juliet, a girl with a troubled past, makes a bet that she can seduce hot new Latin teacher Mr Spencer, a devout Christian.

But while Mr Spencer wrestles with his faith as he tries to resist his growing attraction to Juliet, she's starting to realise that it's become more than just a game for her.

Summer's Edge

He's fighting it but he needs this as much as I do.

When Stewart Walker finds out the girl he kissed is a student at his school he's furious and determined to keep away. But 18-year-old Alice has fallen hard and won't give up. She wants him to teach her body and her mind, even though a relationship is strictly against the rules. He's struggling to resist the attraction despite knowing he could lose his job.

Throughout the illegal raves and festivals of Britain's summer of '92, Alice and Stewart dance closer and closer to the edge.

Available in paperback or eBook from Lulu.com

FORBIDDEN LESSONS

by

Noël Cades

First Printing, 2014

ISBN: 0992501717
ISBN-13: 978-0-9925017-1-6

This book is dedicated to Helen & Charlie

"Verbum dei lucerna"

PART I

Feeling

The fire falls asunder, all is changed,
I am no more a child

Ann Lowell

1. Old and new

Old and new mingling and fighting - it was the smell that always characterised the start of a new term. It swirled around Laura, dragging her in, bringing her back.

The old desks, classrooms, wooden floorboards, dusty library books, the ageing metallic tang of the chemistry lab, the stale remembrance of boiled cabbage in the dining hall. Invaded by the smell of new exercise books, school shoes, fresh paint, gym equipment.

The battle lasted a few days, but old always won. Within a week, all the newness was absorbed into the school. It was too much for anyone or anything to fight against.

New faces. Everyone moved up a year together, but there were always a few girls that left at the end of each year and a handful of new ones that came to replace them. They were the great curiosity. Teachers too. Everyone always hoped that a strict old dragon had left, replaced by a new, younger person with more interesting teaching methods.

"Mr Carlisle has left, gone to run a school in Botswana."

"Mrs Ayers is still here, worse luck! If only I could drop Geography."

"Have you seen the new music rooms?"

Excited chatter at seeing old friends, with the start-of-term homesickness and the reality of the months of grind ahead not yet sinking in.

Laura found her two best friends, Margery and Charlotte. They'd managed to secure a dorm together this term, and so far the fourth bed wasn't occupied. There was always the hope it might remain empty. Charlotte, the sporty one, had wanted to see the hockey pitches so they'd escaped and headed for the grounds. Unpacking could be done later. Even Matron showed lenience on the first day back.

Softened by the golden September light and seen from a distance, the red-brick Victorian school buildings looked temporarily less grim.

"Such a great decision, ditching Geography for German," Charlotte said, stretching her legs out over the thick grass under the copper beech trees that lined one side of the pitches.

"Whoever's teaching it, they can't be as bad as Mrs Ayers," Laura agreed.

"That's hardly a good reason to change subjects," said Margery. She was slightly huffy. "German is an important European language. You're not supposed to take it just to get out of another subject." Margery's father taught modern languages at another school and she was the studious one of the three.

"Don't be so sensitive!" Charlotte said. "We all know it's not a soft option. But I truly could not stick that hag for another year. She deliberately gave me detentions so I'd keep missing practice."

Laura lay back and closed her eyes. The summer was fading fast, nearly gone. The vast expanse of the autumn term, with its growing cold and darkness, lay ahead. The holidays and Christmas, even half-term, were so far away.

Charlotte changed the subject. "Onto more important matters. We need a strategy for combatting Teresa Hubert's vile posse and making sure we grab the hottest Dunks guys for the half term dance."

St Duncan's was the "brother" school to Francis Hall, with pupils from each school occasionally allowed to meet at carefully supervised coeducational social occasions such as school concerts and joint orchestra performances. Teresa Hubert and her friends - or henchwomen, as Charlotte termed them - were a constant irritation. War had broken out in the Fourth form over something long forgotten, but the hostilities endured.

"I heard there's going to be a joint play this year, performed by both schools. Miss Vine managed to get permission from the Headmistress to do Romeo and Juliet for the Christmas production. Sixth formers only though," Margery said.

"How utterly unfair! They're supposed to be busy with A-levels, it should be us," Charlotte retorted. "Miss Vine is such a sweet idiot. I mean what could possibly go wrong? I predict a dozen buns in the oven by curtain up, unless Matron starts doling out the Pill."

Laura laughed. "It won't be that bad. Most of the Dunks boys wouldn't know what to do if it stared them in the face."

"What makes you such an expert?" said Charlotte.

"I'm not. But they're just boys aren't they, most of them, even the sixth formers? I just feel that this summer I've kind of outgrown all that."

Charlotte, who had been lying down as well, sat up and looked at Laura. "Spill!" she said.

"Oh there's nothing to tell. Truly. I kissed one French boy at the hotel disco but my parents were in the next bar, which you know all about because I told you in great detail, and beyond that it was an absolute drought."

"One thing I do think is that Mr Peters will be mightily pissed off," Charlotte said, stretching out once again in the last of the day's sun. Mr Peters was the Head of English and Miss Vine taught drama. The former's seniority and more forceful presence meant that the school play had until now remained entirely his domain. "His casting couch will lie empty."

There were longstanding rumours that Mr Peters seduced sixth form girls, usually by casting them as Juliet or Ophelia in the school play and giving them private acting lessons. Laura doubted - or found herself wanting to doubt the rumours - because she personally thought Mr Peters was repellent. He had thinning grey hair, an over-mannered voice, bad breath and must have been nearly fifty.

But the evidence - albeit technically hearsay by the time it reached Lower School ears - was so extensive and so detailed that even Margery considered it gospel.

"I think we should all be more serious about our studies this year," said Margery. "Boys are a distraction we really don't need." Margery's posture of studiousness masked a lack of confidence and experience when it came to dating. Both Laura and Charlotte knew this, and tried to be tactful.

Charlotte was the tall, attractive athletic one of the three, with her supermodel figure already turning heads wherever she went. Laura's dark blonde hair and amber eyes contributed to her unusual attractiveness. But even Margery, with her frank blue eyes and rose-flushed cheeks, had charms she wasn't yet aware of.

"I think I learn better when there's some fun in my life. One needs a balance," Charlotte said. She had been on dates with three different boys that summer - a record for their group - and still managed to finish her English reading list.

"Just think of what happened to Lucy Martin," Margery said. "I can't think of anything more terrible than that." Lucy Martin was something of a legend in the school, albeit infamous rather than celebrated. She had been in the sixth form a few years ago, a scholarship girl who was tipped to go to Oxford, but she had fallen pregnant and been expelled when the school found out.

"I can think of something far more terrible," said Laura.

"What?"

"Getting back to our dorm and finding Teresa Hubert in the fourth bed. Come on! There's the bell. We may as well not annoy Matron too much on the first evening, if we can help it."

* * *

Happily, the fourth bed remained empty on their return. The dormitory had two beds by the windows at one end, taken by Laura and Charlotte. The other two beds were either side of the door. Margery had taken one of these, as conveniently for all of them she didn't like windows. She had a fear of something looking through at her in the night.

Charlotte bounced on her bed. "Much as I hate school to the bottom of my feet, except for hockey and tennis, I am glad to be back with you guys. Wales was great, but being back home got very dreary." Charlotte's father was extremely strict - her romantic dalliances had only been made possible by a fortnight's stay with her Welsh grandmother. School actually represented more freedom for her in some ways than her home did.

"I wonder if that bed will stay empty?" Laura said.

"I doubt it. They're usually packed to the rafters. Everyone wants to be in Michaelmas House, because of Gi-Gi," Charlotte said. Grace Grant, their housemistress, was regarded as by far the nicest of all the houseparents in the schools. Whitsun House - all the houses were named after liturgical dates for some long-forgotten reason - suffered under the dread rule of the Geography teacher, Mrs Ayers.

"I can't think who's late back, I'm sure I've seen just about everyone," Margery said. She fretted a little. "What if it's a snorer? I couldn't bear if it was a snorer. I really need my sleep this year so I can study properly."

"If you thrashed yourself out at Games a bit more you'd sleep like a log even in a thunderstorm," Charlotte said. Margery was not a sporty girl. Laura was average. Given the choice Laura would have preferred to play something like cricket or even rugby, which she had played with her cousins in the holidays, but these weren't an option at Francis Hall. Two terms of hockey preceded a summer term of athletics and tennis. She had little interest in these so didn't put much effort in.

Laura also dreaded ever getting picked for a sports team - Charlotte's greatest desire - as it meant giving up even more time having to travel miles in the school coach to matches every weekend. Laura preferred to escape with a book on weekends. Charlotte went off with her jolly hockey sticks, Margery put her nose to the grindstone, and Laura read everything from their English texts to smuggled novels forbidden by the school. The three of them enjoyed perfect harmony as a result - not overly living in one another's pockets.

"I shall keep a diary this year," Margery announced. "I think we all should. It's a good way to gather your thoughts and will be interesting for us all to look back on years from now."

"Good girls keep diaries, bad girls don't have time," said Charlotte.

"I might give it a go," Laura said. She had a blank journal that she hadn't yet found a purpose for. She had thought of writing poetry - she was the creative one of the three - but English homework tended to keep them so busy that her inspiration ran out beyond the composition required for class.

"I'll keep a sports diary then." Charlotte had vague ambitions of being a sports commentator. She would have also liked to play for England at hockey, or perhaps javelin, but wasn't yet convinced that she was good enough or that Francis Hall would provide sufficient training. Always the pragmatist and the optimist, she was keeping her options open.

Laura laughed. "I know you, you'll end up just putting match results in with no commentary."

"Maybe. We'll see. If it's awful weather, I'll have more time on my hands," Charlotte said.

2. New Language

He was tall. That was the first thing Laura noticed. He had clear-cut features and had a kind of masterfulness that many new teachers lacked, to their cost. He reminded her of a book she had once read, of a man who "must have done something in life".

She saw Teresa Hubert simpering with her friends across the room, and also realised how good looking he was.

"I'm Mr Rydell," he told them. "I'm from Surrey, I read Modern Languages at Cambridge, I've previously taught at schools in Hertfordshire and Northamptonshire, and my goal is introduce you to German in a way that inspires at least some of you to love the language and its literature as I do."

Concise, factual, straight to the point. Their initial unasked questions all answered. Everyone always wanted to know where a teacher was from and where they had been, in part so they could assess how soft a touch lay before them. "This is my first job" or "I'm new to teaching" were fatal.

"German is more challenging in certain ways than French or Spanish, but also highly rewarding. If you put the effort in, you'll very quickly be able to use basic German on holiday, or to talk with German visitors," he continued. "Hands up who's done Latin?"

Around half the hands went up, including Laura's. Latin was compulsory at Francis Hall for the top set and was the bane of their lives. Mr Rydell's eyes went around the room. When they met hers - it was only for a moment, she felt a sudden jolt. For a split second the rest of the room disappeared, and then he moved on and she felt herself flush and wanted to hide behind her hair. Which she couldn't do, because it was neatly tied back as school rules demanded.

Oh I hope I didn't make an idiot of myself, she thought. Had he noticed? He seemed so much more serious than other teachers. In fact he hadn't even smiled yet.

"Though German isn't as complex as Latin, you will find your studies useful for recognising certain elements of grammar," he explained.

Textbooks were handed out, and opened at the first chapter. Teresa muttered and sniggered something to her friend, then froze as Mr Rydell looked directly at them.

"I would like this to be enjoyable for all of us," he said. "But it is going to be hard work, particularly for those of you taking exams a year early, and will require everyone's full attention." He emphasised these last words while looking at Teresa. There was a faint contempt in his voice, which coming from him seemed more cutting than any direct censure or threat of detention.

The posse at the side of the classroom went white and quiet. There was a crackle of electricity around the room. Rarely did a new teacher assert that they meant business so quickly or so effectively.

The lesson progressed, and Laura was happy to discover that he was a very inspiring teacher. He had a broad depth of knowledge, and had spent considerable time in Germany.

"Are you fluent, Sir?" one girl asked.

"Not natively. Sufficiently for conversation and correspondence," he told her.

When Laura was looking down at a list of basic vocabulary, she had no idea how but she felt his eyes on her. She glanced up, and he held her gaze for a moment, before turning to the blackboard again. She couldn't read his glance at all, but her stomach did the same flip that it had done earlier. Get a grip, she thought. He clearly can't stand foolish schoolgirls, look at how he reacted to Teresa Hubert's giggling.

* * *

"Wow, wasn't he gorgeous but terrifying?!" was the general consensus voiced after the lesson. "I shall totally dread German!"

"Did you see how harsh he was towards Teresa?"

"I wouldn't want to get on his bad side."

"What a shame that someone that looks like that has to be so strict and serious!"

Laura didn't think so at all, but she kept her opinion to herself. Despite the steel grip of discipline that he maintained the class in, she had enjoyed her first German lesson. And she kept remembering the feeling in her stomach when he looked at her.

Normally she would have confided this to Charlotte and Margery but something held her back. Her reaction to the new teacher seemed so out of step with everyone else's that she needed more time to analyse it. Her new journal would be the perfect place.

Lunch was awful. Laura predicted that once their tuckboxes, which helpfully supplemented school food in the first weeks of term, were empty, she would actually lose weight. She never understood how Charlotte could stuff down so much over-boiled stodge with apparent gusto. Exercise surely couldn't make someone's tastebuds that undiscriminating. But even Margery, albeit more slowly, steadily ate her way through soggy cabbage, dumplings and the horridly gristly beef stew.

You were required to finish your plate at Francis Hall, and thank goodness for Charlotte who could hoover up anything that Laura couldn't bear to touch. Often quite gratefully. Swapping food had to be done on the sly of course, but so far they had got away with it.

"You'll fade away if you don't eat," Margery warned her.

"I would eat, quite happily, but I just can't bear school food," Laura said. "I wish we could have packed lunches, or a canteen. I'll have to eke out my tuckbox like starvation rations."

"If only you could do Home Economics you could smuggle yourself some more provisions," Charlotte said. Only lower set girls did Home Economics: those that weren't considered bright enough for Latin, extra Maths and a second modern language.

"Perhaps I can bribe one of them to make me flapjacks. A homework swap maybe," Laura said.

"You can eat apple pie can't you?" asked Charlotte.

"The apple, not the gluggy custard and crust," Laura said.

"Well here, have my apple part at least then," Charlotte offered generously. "You'll need your strength for Games this afternoon."

* * *

It was a beautiful afternoon to be out on the hockey pitch. Clear and a comfortable temperature, it was also nice to escape the classroom. Maths had been absolutely horrendous and they were all sure they were going to fail Physics.

Laura felt herself sinking back into the timetable, the routine. She couldn't fight against it, none of them could. School was all consuming and all absorbing. Every hour of their day was arranged and decided for them save some precious, cherished free time on Saturday evenings and Sunday after chapel.

Miss Partridge was the head Games mistress though other teachers took part in supervising sports as well. This term she had something different to announce.

"Those of you who don't make the squad this year will only play hockey two afternoons a week. The third afternoon will be cross country, in rotation depending on your group."

There was a groan at this from some girls, and Margery's face blanched. She hated hockey enough as it was, but the prospect of cross country running overwhelmed her with terror. "I'll be ok," Laura whispered. "We'll get through it. We'll find short cuts."

"Laura Cardew, no chattering or you'll get a demerit," ordered Miss Partridge.

Laura felt too anxious for Margery to care, but she obeyed. I'll have to make sure I don't make the squad, she thought. Absolutely no way could they leave poor Margery to suffer cross country by herself. There was no question that Charlotte wouldn't make the squad for their age group as well as the actual team selected for matches, so that left Laura having to sacrifice for their friend. It was a bit of a shame as truth be told she didn't mind hockey, but at least cross country would only be for one afternoon a week. It might even be interesting if the route took them out of the school grounds, she thought, trying to find a silver lining.

* * *

That night they sat down dutifully with their diaries, after the two hours of homework were finished. Supper was at six then it was back to the house for homework from seven to nine, then bed by nine-thirty for Lower School girls. Sixth formers enjoyed marginally more freedom - an extra hour of leisure before their bedtime - but they had so much more homework that they tended to use it all for study anyway.

If you were quick getting ready for bed, you had up to thirty minutes before lights out. This had now been decreed Diary Time.

"Dear Diary..." Laura began, then stopped. "How are we supposed to do this?" she asked. "Like Samuel Pepys, or like Anne Frank, as though we were writing to someone?"

"I'm writing mine as though I was the sports correspondent for the BBC," Charlotte said.

"You can do it however you like," Margery told her. "I'm writing mine as a simple, historic account."

"I have no idea what I'm going to write on non-sports days, as every day and week is basically the same here. I can hardly keep writing 'Double Maths was awful, Liver and Onions again for Supper'," Charlotte said.

Laura decided that "Dear Diary" would be adequate.

"Dear Diary. The world changed today. I'm not sure if it was coming back to school and starting another year. Everything seemed the same yesterday, like it would be the same as it was last year, and the same for ever more. And now I'm not sure of anything at all."

All she could think of, as she closed the journal and lay in bed, was a pair of penetrating grey eyes.

3. Exchanging glances

They sat in straight, silent rows one either side of the school chapel, listening to the Headmistress's address. The staff sat on the pews at the furthest end by the altar, and Laura looked for Mr Rydell. He was on the same side as Laura but several rows in front so she could only distantly see the side and back of his head.

The first assembly of term was held on Tuesday, because its timeslot in the first morning back was used to brief new girls. The first Monday was usually so chaotic that extra time was needed anyway to get everyone to the right classrooms. There were always changes from the previous year, sometimes at the last minute. This term the History and Geography classrooms had been inexplicably swapped around, and the new Chemistry lab still had wet paint so a temporary room had had to be found.

"Now I'd like to welcome our new staff, I hope you will all help them feel at home at Francis Hall," Mrs Grayson said. A widow with steely grey hair and military bearing, she had an absolute command of the school. She taught Maths but only to the sixth form.

"I'd like to introduce Miss Quayle, who'll be filling Mr Carlisle's much-missed shoes in Biology." Miss Quayle half stood and gave a sort of nod. She looked rather like a quail,

Laura thought, she was shortish with dowdy brown hair and clothes.

"Miss Wingrove joins Mr Peters' English department," the Headmistress continued. Miss Wingrove looked more interesting, in her early thirties, fair haired, intelligent. She had a nice smile. Laura hoped they'd get her rather than Mr Peters. They hadn't had English yet so she didn't know whom had been allotted.

"And finally Mr Rydell will be teaching German, following Frau Goettner's return to Hamburg."

There was a rustle of interest among the rows on the opposite side as the new German teacher stood momentarily, the majority of girls not yet having seen him. He was certainly the most attractive male member of staff by a long stretch. Not the youngest perhaps - Mr Poynter who taught History was under twenty-five, but he was short with a round, boyish face and owlish glasses. And fey Mr Lanaway in Art was too odd for words. Rare were the hearts that fluttered in either of their classrooms.

Then there were various part time music masters, some of whom were younger than thirty, but unless you played a specific instrument you would never see them. Beyond that, most teachers were elderly males or female.

All in all the school appeared to take care to choose its male teachers from the ranks of the romantically untouchable in Laura's view. Ironic perhaps that the only one crossing the line seemed to be horrid old Mr Peters. Either way, Mr Rydell was an aberration.

Charlotte grinned at Laura and whispered: "just wait until they see what Rydell's like in class!"

"He wasn't so bad," Laura whispered back.

"He'll knock Peters off his perch with the sixth form," Charlotte said, then quickly closed her mouth as she spied a prefect glaring at her.

The organ strummed up, and the final hymn played. Laura sang without really thinking about the words. Francis Hall promised a "Christian education" but it rather washed over her, she wasn't one of the earnest girls who went to confirmation classes and Christian Union. Neither, fortunately, were Charlotte or Margery.

Charlotte was an avowed atheist, Margery professed a sort of inactive belief, and Laura didn't really know or care. There was too much else to think about and learn. Religion just buzzed along in the background, always there, more boring than offensive.

* * *

They didn't have German that day but Laura saw Mr Rydell in the dining hall at lunch. She thought he looked back at her, but before she could be sure they had to turn around to say Grace and start the meal, which left her with her back to him. She could hardly crane around again and look at him.

She felt the changed world again. For a fleeting moment, she and the German teacher were the most important people in the world and everyone else in the room was a grey mush.

"Snap out of it, you're daydreaming again," Charlotte said. "I asked you if it was History or Latin first this afternoon." Charlotte was hopeless with timetables unless they concerned Games practice or matches.

"Latin."

"Good. I've decided to try and enjoy Latin this term," Charlotte said.

This was startling coming from Charlotte. Even Margery raised her eyebrows.

"We're stuck with it, so I thought we should make the best of it. Maybe if we managed to get on top of it it wouldn't seem so awful. Last year it was the utter drag and dread of the week to me, and it put me off my game," Charlotte explained.

"So is this a resolution for all of us?" Laura asked.

"If you like. It will probably be easier as a group effort."

* * *

True to her word, Charlotte displayed a new and disturbing diligence in Latin. She answered questions, concentrated throughout the entire class, and even suggested to old Mr Tyrrell that they do slightly more than the usual amount of translation so they could reach the end of a particular poem. He agreed in happy surprise, and everyone else groaned.

"You'll get death threats if you keep this up," Laura warned.

"Oh they'll all handle it," Charlotte said. "They'll thank me once exam time comes."

"Not from them - from us. I don't mind paying a bit more attention to Latin homework, but I wasn't bargaining on extra lines. If Margery doesn't end up strangling you in your bed then I will." Laura was still slightly bewildered by Charlotte's Latin resolution. Some secret lay at the bottom of it, she was quite certain, and she would find out in time what it was.

"At least we're through all the grammar this year. All the conjugation tables and so on." Last year had progressed through noun declensions, verb conjugations, tenses and voices. There was endless memorisation every homework, and tests at the start of every lesson.

Every few weeks had seemed to required them to double their knowledge. Re-learning everything in the passive had been bad enough. But when Mr Tyrrell introduced the subjunctive they had nearly collapsed in despair.

"We're not really through it all though, only the testing," Margery said. "I still struggle to remember them all." It was an honest admission as languages were Margery's thing.

* * *

Happily they had the new female teacher for English, though she explained that classes would alternate with Mr Peters this year. Miss Wingrove was as pleasant and as interesting as she appeared and Laura mentally ticked English as a look-forward-to lesson.

With the plays taken up by Miss Vine and Mr Peters, Miss Wingrove's side project that year was going to be a poetry recital. "All kinds, not just Keats and Shakespeare. Your own works if you like."

Laura liked this idea. Margery detested it. Charlotte was indifferent. She had a good voice and plenty of confidence but no real interest in the arts. It was no issue to her whether she took part or not, though if Laura did, she'd probably give it a go. "Maybe you could write something for me, and I'll recite it," she suggested to Margery.

* * *

Once again they scurried to finish in the bathroom so they could pick up their pens for the diary writing.

"Should we read one another's work every week or so?" Margery asked. Laura blanched.

"God no," said Charlotte.

"Why? Are you writing horrid things about me?" Margery asked.

"No. I simply don't want to read your entries, I suspect they'll bore me to tears," Charlotte said. Laura silently thanked her. Right now her journal was her only confessional. She had craved writing it since the morning, even though she didn't plan to write very much.

"Perhaps we can read our favourite excerpts aloud once a month," she suggested to mollify Margery. She also didn't want Margery peeking. Laura wasn't sure what was going on with herself right now, but it felt like she had entered another dimension.

They were running out of time before lights out, so they hurriedly picked up their pens.

"Dear Diary. I have never felt so alone. I feel that something has taken me away from my friends, and put me in a new reality that they can never understand. It's like the rest of the world has vanished. Is anyone else feeling this way? Is everyone? I can't be the only one. I had a crush on Nick James all last year but it was nothing like this. What do I do? Will it go away? I wish you could answer me."

4. Skipping Lunch

In their next German lesson Mr Rydell remarked on Laura's handwriting when he handed back their corrected translations. "Fine handwriting, what pen do you use?" The neutrality of his tone made it more like an observation than a compliment.

Laura did have good handwriting. A couple of years ago a history teacher had held optional calligraphy classes, and she had tried and enjoyed them. She had since practiced incorporating some of the features in her regular writing.

"It's a cursive Italic nib."

"Does it slow you down?" he asked.

"Not really." She tended to use a different nib in exams, when faster writing was required. But homework was generally written out carefully and it took her no longer with the Italic nib than with a rounded one.

He nodded, looking directly at her. He held the glance just a fraction longer than necessary, and for a moment she thought he was going to ask her something further, before he moved to the next desk. We connected, she thought. Or am I reading too much into this? She felt shaky from merely speaking with him.

"Are you ok?" Charlotte whispered to her.

"I'm fine, why?"

"You look odd. Pale. Like when you fainted in gym." A couple of terms ago Laura had been coming down with a bad virus and had fainted during a gym lesson.

She pinched her cheeks to flush them, and smiled at Charlotte. "Better?" Then she looked up and saw Mr Rydell looking at them both, his eyebrows raised slightly, and blushed for real. Fortunately he didn't censure them for talking and the lesson continued.

* * *

Morning break was twenty minutes between lessons, which they tended to spend in the courtyard unless something had been forgotten for the next class.

The "court" was the centre point of the various buildings at Francis Hall. It had a flowerbed surrounded by a low wall - red brick like the surrounding architecture - that was convenient to sit on. Different groups of girls might have appeared to be seated randomly, but there was in fact a distinct and unspoken understanding on who was supposed to sit where, based on social hierarchy.

Charlotte, with her confidence and figure and her rumoured success with boys, had risen the ranks over the past year, taking Laura and Margery with her. This elevated them to a coveted position on the west wall.

No one ever sat where they were not supposed to sit. Laura always marvelled at the order of it. "What would happen if we simply went and sat on the east wall one day?" she said.

"Prefects would kick us off and be on our backs all term," Charlotte said.

"It's idiotic though, it's just a wall. I mean if we went and sat on the steps with the fourth formers, would anyone care? It's not like it's a rule."

"Some things matter more than rules."

* * *

Laura dreaded lunch more than supper at the moment. Mrs Ayers was assigned to their table that week, and her gimlet eye made it nearly impossible to swap unwanted food or smuggle it into a pocket. Worse still, it was liver today - grey-green and scummy - and Laura didn't think she could bear to even taste it.

Skipping lunch without reason was a severe offence, so she went to the school nurse's room to try and contrive an illness and get a pass. A sore throat, requiring a liquid diet? Nausea? She had to be careful, because too many attempts to avoid meals might put her under even more scrutiny. If they thought she had an eating disorder she would be done for, with a teacher breathing down her neck every meal.

The nurse was in a kind mood that day. "It's liver today, isn't it?" she said, when Laura started to invent symptoms.

"Yes." There was no point lying. "I honestly have a healthy appetite, but I just can't do it, I really can't."

"You don't look underweight. I don't want you getting that way though, so be careful. You can have a note today, but it won't be possible every Tuesday."

Laura thanked her.

"What about registering as vegetarian? Would your parents agree?" the nurse suggested.

It was an idea. Laura tried to think of meat dishes she would actually miss. Beyond cottage pie, there weren't many. "I'll write to them this evening." She wondered why she hadn't thought of it before.

Thanks to the note she could safely avoid the dining hall altogether, and so she decided to sit and read in a sunny spot overlooking the tennis courts. For some time she lost herself in Rebecca, one of the approved novels in the school library.

"Isn't it lunch time?" She heard a voice behind her and froze. It was him. He seemed even taller outdoors in the sun, his shoulders broad, forming his body into a triangle shape as it narrowed to his hips. He looked so strong. She wondered wildly what it would be like to be crushed in his arms.

"I have a sick note."

"Are you ill?" She realised there was actually concern in his voice, which made her feel embarrassed, particularly given her very healthy train of thought.

"Actually no, but it's liver today." This time he raised his eyebrows fully, and for a moment she wondered if he would smile, but he didn't.

"I haven't yet experienced that delicacy."

"I hope you manage to enjoy it when you do," she said. He continued to look at her, his gaze inscrutable, and then - still unsmiling - he left.

* * *

"Where were you at lunch?" Charlotte demanded, as they went to the Maths classroom.

"I managed to get a note."

"You're lucky you were looking pale before. It was even more of a struggle than usual, it really stank," Charlotte said.

"Actually Nurse guessed it was liver, but let me off anyway which was nice. She's suggested going vegetarian."

"That's still pretty awful you know. Very dull - grated cheddar one day, and a hard boiled egg the next. And you'd still be stuck with cabbage," Charlotte warned.

"At least I could eat that."

"If you did diabetes you could probably get off puddings too," said Margery. "But I think you'd need an actual doctor's note for that."

"And syringes and things." It wasn't a great idea.

* * *

The last lesson that day was Double Art - it was always two lessons back to back, due to the time taken setting up and clearing up. Margery hated art, but Charlotte and Laura regarded it more as fun than work.

Today they had to practice shading gradients with different hardnesses of pencil, then sketch a still life object from the art room. Laura chose a terracotta vase, made and abandoned by a long-ago sixth former. The Lower School didn't get to use either of the pottery wheels.

Mr Lanaway was in despair trying to help Margery. He was a very thin, pale man and a brilliant sculptor. Margery simply had no sense of light and shade. The fact that she despised art, considering it a waste of time that could be spent more profitably on academic subjects, didn't help either.

Having finished her sketch Laura wandered around the pottery room, looking at damp lumps of clay-in-progress under cloth on various trolleys. Classroom discipline was quite different in Art, they were encouraged to explore what other people had been making. She saw that one class - probably A-Level Ceramics - had been trying to sculpt human figures.

There was a huge block of clay on the table, ready for Mr Lanaway to cut up. It was solid, square and dark grey. Laura suddenly imagined pulling a form from it: sinewy shoulders, flat pectorals, a strong, well shaped neck. She wanted to make something she could touch.

"Sir, could you teach us how to sculpt this term?"

A lot of girls didn't like ceramics because of the sticky, muddy feel of clay, and getting it stuck under their fingernails. Art in terms of drawing or painting was considered less messy and physical. So it was an unusual delight for the art teacher to get such a request. Mr Lanaway was also delighted to find interest shown in his own area of talent.

"By all means. We'll start next week, those that are interested."

* * *

"Dear Diary, he stopped to talk to me today. Did he stay longer than he needed to? I feel like this must be all in my head, but it's as if there is no one else in the world when he's there. I have to get over this. There's the whole of the sixth form before me."

5. Lost in translation

Charlotte was no fool. She knew she had put backs up through her new zeal for Latin and that it would be socially strategic to make amends.

She put her hand up in class. "Sir, I was wondering if it might help bring our Caesar text to life if we visited the Welchester Roman Museum one day? Perhaps on a Sunday afternoon?"

Seeing the Latin teacher's expression start to open to the idea she fired the killer shot. "And of course it could be very useful to those of us thinking of doing Latin for A-Levels."

Fewer and fewer girls every year took Latin in the sixth form, much to Mr Tyrrell's despair. The prospect of having Charlotte and some of these other bright girls in his class next year was the perfect carrot.

"I should think that would be a splendid idea!" he said. One of the girls in the back row muffled a snigger. Only Mr Tyrrell could get excited about a town museum.

What Mr Tyrrell didn't know but what Charlotte and every other girl was keenly aware of was that St Duncan's boys were taken to Welchester Museum nearly every weekend, as their school was in the same town. Even if there wasn't a contingent at the museum itself that day, there was a good chance of seeing some of the sixth form boys down at the shops.

"I'll see about getting the school coach for next weekend," he told them.

Charlotte's crown of popularity was restored.

* * *

"If only we could wear mufti," Laura sighed. The days they were allowed out of school in regular clothes were extremely rare. Francis Hall's school uniform, which was nearly head-to-toe maroon wool in the winter term, was not considered fetching by any of them.

"I'm going to borrow Mary Rudge's skirt," said Charlotte. Mary Rudge was the shortest girl in Michaelmas house.

"But she's half your height!" said Margery.

"Exactly. Her skirt will be above my knees, and if Gi-Gi or anyone else tries to get me to roll it down it won't be possible. I'll put it on it at the last minute so there's no time to change." Rolling skirts up at the waist was a popular way to shorten them but you could get a demerit point if you were unlucky.

"We can manage some make up too, if we put it on in the coach," Laura said. "Depending on who's coming to supervise, of course."

"It will probably be one of the teachers who can drive the coach if Jenkins is off," Margery pointed out. Jenkins was the school handyman who doubled up as a coach driver, but a few of the teaching staff also held bus licences.

"That's ok then, it's all the gimpy ones that do that. They never notice stuff like that. Nor will Tyrrell."

* * *

They had Double German that day which Laura had been waiting for all week. She had obsessed about her perfecting her homework while trying to conceal her efforts from the others. Mr Rydell was wearing a tie with grey stripes today that matched his eyes.

Laura had long ago learnt to suppress laughter by digging her nails into her thumbs. Getting a fit of the giggles in certain situations was a lethal route to detentions and other punishments, but sometimes it was hard to help it. Particularly when the choirmaster's toupée slipped while conducting a particularly vigorous anthem in chapel.

Now she used her nails to try and control her lurching stomach and the blushes she was certain kept coming to her face whenever she caught his eye. Which she was sure was more than normal, but was it because she kept looking at him too much? She tried to concentrate on staring down at her textbook.

Teresa Hubert had tried quite a different homework strategy to Laura. She had deliberately messed hers up so she could beg Mr Rydell for extra help. This met with short shrift.

"If you require more study time I can arrange it with your housemistress for Saturday afternoon, and you can redo this week's exercises and give them to me on Monday," he told her.

Teresa looked horrified. This was practically a voluntary detention.

"No, I won't need that, I have enough time in the evenings," she said.

"Be sure you use it."

He turned away from her and started on the subject of German's compound nouns. The textbook gave some examples, and Mr Rydell wrote another couple of unfeasibly long examples on the blackboard which he assured them were genuine words.

Laura looked up. "Are they like Old English words?" she said.

He was surprised by this. "Are you studying Old English?"

"Mr Peters showed us some Anglo-Saxon verse at the end of last term."

"Those tend to be called kennings, they're used in a more figurative, poetic sense, but yes. German shares certain features with older forms of English than it does with more modern English." He smiled at her. It was the first time she had ever seen him smile, certainly at her, and it dazzled her. To keep herself focused she dug her nails into her thumbs so hard they nearly bled.

* * *

The Geography teacher Mrs Ayers loathed Michaelmas girls. Some years ago she had applied to be housemistress of what was considered to be the best house in the choicest location but had been turned down. She had later managed to secure the equivalent position at the smaller Whitsun House, but the rejection still rankled.

Woe betide any Michaelmas girls with lost garters or untidy hair around Mrs Ayers. Whilst she might show leniency towards Advent or Lammas girls and always turned the blindest of eyes to her own Whitsun inmates, anyone under Grace Grant's care could expect the full force of her venom in a slew of demerits. No wonder she was nicknamed "The Axe".

"Your socks are down - both of them. Double demerits!" she snapped at Charlotte when she passed them in the courtyard.

"Oh come on, that's unfair, it's never more than one for both, they're not separate offences," Charlotte protested.

"Would you like a third demerit point for answering back?"

Charlotte had no choice but to bite her tongue. Three demerit points meant Saturday detention, which meant no hockey matches. Which was not only disappointing but would bring the wrath of Miss Partridge upon her as well.

When the Geography teacher had finally gone the others offered their sympathy. "I'm almost surprised she didn't just give you the third," Laura said.

"I'm not. Giving someone three points in a single day, so that they get detention, might be scrutinised. It's pretty harsh. Gi-Gi might even protest it," Margery said.

"Still not worth the risk though. I absolutely have to play in the match against Everleigh College or Hubert will get my position as right wing and even keep it if she sucks up enough."

* * *

Laura had written to her parents but it would be a wait until their permission slip for her dietary change came through. Until then she was doomed to force down the foul school chow, doing her best to slip what she could to Charlotte. She had tried secreting something awful in her blazer pocket the other day which she had pre-lined with A4 paper.

But it leaked everywhere and she got a scolding from Matron, who ironically thought she was smuggling out extra food to eat later. "You finish your meal at the table and nowhere else. Snacking only makes girls fat."

Thank God for her tuckbox. Maybe she could try to replenish its stores in Welchester. She hoped a diet of predominantly Mars Bars wouldn't make her break out in acne.

* * *

"Dear Diary, he smiled at me today. Me and only me. It felt like the sun came out. Oh I wish we had German every day. I wish every single lesson was German. Why can't I be in the sixth form already, doing German for A-Levels? They get to see him daily, sometimes twice. Whereas I'm languishing on starvation rations."

6. In the rain

It poured that afternoon: wet and grey and grim under a leaden sky. One of the staff had asked Laura to fetch a pile of books from one of the English classrooms at break-time, not realising it was raining so heavily. Laura obliged as you often got bonus points this way. These would help offset Mrs Ayers' endless demerits towards the overall House total.

As good luck or ill Fate would have it - she wasn't sure which, afterwards - she came back up around the corner to collide straight with The Axe. It was a pure accident - not helped by the rain in her hair and eyes - and Laura slipped up on the wet path and fell, with the books scattering. The dumpy Geography teacher maintained her own balance quite well. Less so her temper.

"You stupid girl!" she shrieked. "Why can't you look where you're going? You've bruised me and damaged all those books. A triple demerit and detention this Saturday!"

Laura, whose knee was throbbing with pain, could only look up at her in misery.

"I think that may be unfairly harsh, it's wet and slippery and she was carrying a large load." It was Mr Rydell. Amid her shock, Laura braced herself for The Axe's fury. She would never suffer to be corrected by a newer and thus junior member of staff.

"She should look where she's going when carrying valuable school property. She crashed into me quite deliberately! These Michaelmas girls have no consideration or discipline."

"With respect, I witnessed what happened and it was a clear accident. I would be happy to make a report as such to the Head," he told her. He had lowered his voice as though he was only addressing the other teacher, but Laura could still hear. Realising her defeat, Mrs Ayers stormed off. "Now let's get out of the rain. Are you hurt?" he asked, turning to Laura.

"I'm fine." She clearly wasn't, her knee was grazed and bleeding. Her blood was mixing with the rain, streaking down her leg and making it look worse than it was.

"I expect you'll need to see the nurse for that. I'll carry the books for you. Where were you taking them?" Laura told him. "Very well." They picked them up together.

She turned to head towards the nurse's room, which was back in the direction of the English rooms.

Then he called after her.

"Laura?"

She turned back. "Yes sir?"

"I'd like to see you in my classroom after lessons finish, if you have time before prep."

There was usually a break of around twenty minutes between classes and first prep, when they did an hour of homework before supper.

"Of course." Her mind was racing in anticipation. She wished he hadn't seen her like this, her hair a bedraggled mess, sprawled clumsily on the ground. And what did he want to speak with her about?

* * *

Laura could not concentrate at all in the final two classes that day. The first was Maths, to which she was late anyway due to visiting the nurse's room. Fortunately you always got a note and there was a large bandage on her knee to bear additional witness. Teresa Hubert muttered something about "clumsy clot" and sniggered with her friends, but it washed off Laura entirely.

Finally it was History and she felt bad when Mr Poynter twice asked her something and she hadn't heard what she said. He was such a nice, earnest man. "I am sorry, sir, I think I'm a bit distracted by my knee." He was all kindness when she pointed out her bandage though Teresa rolled her eyes.

Charlotte and Margery were dying to find out what was up with her, but she didn't have time to tell them. She also didn't have time to fix her appearance. Laura was the unofficial beautician of the three: she could manage quite spectacular feats with talcum powder, charcoal smuggled from the art room and even fountain pen ink, since actual make up was banned at Francis Hall.

But today she had no choice but to rush off, with her bedraggled-now-dried hair and undecorative bandage.

* * *

The modern languages classrooms were in a newer block behind and below the dining hall. Each classroom opened from the exterior wall, which was glass paned from ceiling to floor, giving them plenty of natural light but creating rather a goldfish bowl effect. It was easy to be distracted in class by other people walking outside, though no one should be around at this hour.

Mr Rydell was behind his desk arranging some stacks of exercise books. The door was open so she couldn't knock but she didn't want to walk right in. She hovered momentarily, but fortunately he looked up almost immediately and told her to come in.

"Have a seat," he said, indicating one of the desks in the front row.

"I wanted to speak with you because I was concerned about what I saw this afternoon," he said, getting straight to the point. "Is there any reason that Mrs Ayers would be so angered with you?"

"It's not me in particular," Laura said. She noticed that the rain had also left his hair more dishevelled. It fell over his forehead slightly, making him look younger. She wondered how old he really was.

"Is she always like that?"

Laura didn't want to come across as sneaky or whiny, but neither could she lie. No one else in the school would paint The Axe in a flattering light if he asked them.

"I think sometimes things can get competitive with House points," she said.

"House points?"

"She runs a different house and sometimes there's rivalry over points." She hoped it didn't sound as stupid to him as it did to her. The sad fact was that it was actually true.

He didn't say anything, just looked at her. She felt pressured to continue.

"I know it sounds petty, but things get like that here. It's her whole life, here." As she said it she felt a touch of empathy with The Axe for the first time, and a kind of shuddering dread at a life that would turn someone to be that way. "You know what school is like. People get… institutionalised." It was a word she had heard her father use to describe the prison service but she thought it fitted here too.

Mr Rydell raised his eyebrows.

"Oh I didn't mean you!" Laura said in horror. "Not everyone. Just some people, some teachers. Especially with it being a boarding school and so... closed in."

"It's all right," he told her. "I do know what you mean, it's easy for teaching staff to get that way. And quite remarkable how well you understand."

He had called her remarkable. It gave her courage. "Why did you become a teacher then?"

He looked at her, and for the second time ever that she could remember, he smiled. It made her feel warm inside. "Truthfully? For the holidays."

"The holidays?"

"Don't mistake me, I enjoy teaching and find it extremely rewarding. But I wanted a career where I would have plenty of time to myself. An office job with four weeks a year doesn't allow for much travel, or taking sabbaticals for research."

"What about a university position?" Laura asked.

"Academia was on the cards. Still is," he said. "But you have much less choice, at least initially, over where you might end up. School teaching lets me more or less pick and choose what area of the country I end up in. Even overseas."

The prospect of him leaving them to go overseas was awful. She hoped it would never happen. She was already thinking of taking German A-Level if she did well this year.

"So how do you cope with it?" he asked. "Being so closed in?"

"Mainly I read. There are places you can find where you can be undisturbed."

"Like by the tennis courts?" He was referring to the other day, when he had found her skipping lunch.

"That's one place. A lot of nicer places are out-of-bounds." She didn't mention that she frequented these nearly as much, but being caught with nothing but a book was a pretty minor offence. Cigarettes or alcohol, more usual reasons for breaching the bounds, were the serious sins.

It was getting late, and the bell sounded for prep. "You'd better go," he said. "Thank you for coming."

* * *

If she had struggled to concentrate in classes, her mind was absolutely whirling now. This was going to be the least productive prep ever. And then it was going to be completely frustrating at supper having Charlotte and Margery grill her in front of everyone.

Charlotte nudged her elbow. "Where have you been?!" she had written at the top of her exercise book.

Laura glanced around the room to see where Miss Quayle was. The new Biology teacher was supervising early prep that evening and she took her duties rather zealously. She wasn't as bad as the Axe but she was planting herself firmly on the wrong side of the popularity fence among the girls, compared to Miss Wingrove and Mr Rydell who had landed on the good side. She was already getting called The Quail as well.

"Wait until tonight," she wrote back. "Supper too un-private." Was that even a word? Once Charlotte had read it, Laura quickly erased it.

Margery looked at them from across the table. She was hopeless at reading upside down. "Tonight," Charlotte mouthed at her. Margery frowned. "TONIGHT" Charlotte mouthed more obviously, then quickly bent her head down as Laura nudged to warn her that Miss Quayle was approaching.

Supper passed quite quickly and being forced to talk about other things was helpful. After the meal and by the time they had got back to the house for prep, Laura had quite gathered her thoughts. Nothing had really happened, when she had had time to think about it. The turmoil was all in her mind, and she wasn't willing to share that with the others. Yet. But they would enjoy the incident with The Axe.

* * *

"So?!" Charlotte was bouncing on her bed in anticipation. "What have you been up to this afternoon? Getting into accidents and rushing off. But that's not it. It's the cagey look on your face. Spill everything."

"It really isn't much to be honest," Laura said. She related the incident with The Axe, which they drank up avidly. Laura was a good storyteller, and conjured up an image of the furious Geography teacher very vividly.

"I can't believe Mr Rydell came to your rescue like that! How amazing. And how wonderful, if it means open warfare between the two of them. She must hate him already given she lost so many pupils from Geography to German," Charlotte said.

"But what about after History?" Margery asked. "You still haven't explained that."

"Mr Rydell just wanted to check I was ok. It was nothing, really."

"NOTHING?!" The other two practically turned on Laura physically. "You absolutely cannot say that the most fascinating teacher to ever enter these hallowed halls rescuing you from The Axe and then requesting your personal presence is 'nothing'."

"I wouldn't described them as hallowed," said Laura, trying to change the subject.

"Well what did he say?" Margery asked.

Laura gave a brief account, much more concise than her report of the accident. "Honestly it was very mundane. He was just shocked how nasty she is, I think. Who wouldn't be?"

Charlotte rolled her eyes and went back out to the bathroom for something she had forgotten.

Margery looked at her rather anxiously. "You know that he looks at you sometimes," she said.

Laura's stomach lurched over but she didn't respond. Margery was strange when it came to observation. She was frustratingly obtuse about everything most of the time even if it was right before her nose. Then once in a while she would notice something - really subtle yet often quite significant - that had passed the others by.

"He looks at all of us," she said. "Probably to make sure we're not messing around."

"Dear Diary, I don't what to make of today. I don't if this is normal, or if I'm trying to read something into it because I want to. I should be excited about the Museum on Sunday, but all I can think of is the endless wait for the weekend to be over and it to be Monday and German again."

7. The new girl

Mr Peters did not like Miss Wingrove. She had not been his first choice - or in fact his choice at all - for the English department. But she had been personally recommended by a close acquaintance of Mrs Grayson, who had decided to go above Mr Peters' head on this occasion. The Headmistress was aware of the rumours surrounding the Head of English, but for as long as he kept getting a contingent of girls into Oxford and Cambridge each year she was under pressure not to disturb the waters. After all, no girl nor parent had ever complained.

So Mrs Grayson had decided that a sensible young woman like Miss Wingrove would be a useful addition to Mr Peter's department, someone whom the girls might feel comfortable approaching if there were indeed any issues. Someone who also might be trusted - at some point - to keep her eyes open.

Mr Peters did not know any of this but the appointment alone was enough to rankle him. He had taken to calling her "Miss Winsome" sarcastically in his mind, and once or twice it had slipped out in class. The Lower School assumed it meant he fancied the new teacher and found it hilarious. The Sixth Form were a little more worldly wise and read his tone more accurately. Unfortunately for Mr Peters it only increased their liking of and loyalty towards the new teacher, rather than encouraging them to have any warmer feeling towards the Head of English.

"Sir? Sir? I've forgotten my Merchant of Venice. Can I run back and get it?"

Irritated, he nodded. He wasn't going to wait for the child. He couldn't even remember her name, she wasn't particularly bright or of any other interest to him. The girl, who was Mary Rudge, ran out to fetch the forgotten book.

The Head of English was indeed having a difficult year. The school play being handed over to that simpering Miss Vine - for that foolish experiment with St Duncan's - had enraged him. Quite apart from the fact that it was a huge obstacle to his customary private acting lessons, the sixth form girls would have their heads filled with pimply schoolboys. Eyeing the Lower School form in front of him, he idly wondered if he should take a leaf from Nabokov and set his sights a little younger this year.

Charlotte Bevan looked older than her years, with her tall, shapely figure. She was also intelligent and spirited, qualities he admired. Her friend Laura Cardew piqued his interest slightly as well. Still waters, he thought. But neither girl was truly his type. He liked a darker, more Mediterranean appearance. The "Dark Lady" of Shakespeare's sonnets as he rather foolishly liked to think.

"We'll read around the class. Charlotte, you'll read Antonio." Having an attractive girl taking a male lead always gave him a frisson. "Laura, Portia." Teresa Hubert scowled at this, for she had wanted to be the heroine. He designated other roles. "I shall read Shylock," he proclaimed. Mr Peters always gave himself a character role, he adored the sound of his own voice.

The lesson progressed, little Mary Rudge slipped in again almost unnoticed, and had to work out which page they were on from her neighbour. Charlotte and Laura had discovered there was a character called "Old Gobbo" which had given them a fit of the giggles. Charlotte kept having to cough to suppress her laughter as she spoke her lines and Mr Peters was getting progressively more irritated. It didn't help that whenever Charlotte calmed down, Laura would murmur the offending name under her breath, setting Charlotte off again.

"I don't know what you both found so funny," said Margery, when the lesson was finally over and they were outside. The other two had tears in their eyes, and had been doubled over laughing. Laura's thumbs were dented all over from her nails.

"I don't know either - it was just the mood," said Charlotte, regaining her composure.

"Bit creepy Peters giving you Antonio," Laura commented. "He always puts his pets in the lead roles. I hope you're not going to be his thing this term."

"You were Portia, you can hardly comment."

"It's not the same with the female roles. He had Judith McLeod read Titania in A Midsummer Night's Dream last year, and she's as plain as punch."

Margery, who had been given the prominent role of Hermia in that play, felt privately affronted.

* * *

It was the first cross-country running session that afternoon for the girls who hadn't made the hockey squad. Laura was slightly sad to have flaked out but Margery was so grateful to her that she didn't regret it for long.

As anticipated, the route took them inside the perimeter of the school grounds, all around the hockey pitches and on the edge of the wasteland area that led down to the strictly out-of-bounds brook. Miss Vine was supervising, but she planned to ride her bicycle back and forth so she could check on the stragglers as easily as the front runners. She was also not in peak fitness herself.

We'll all be stragglers, thought Laura. Just look at this crowd.

Miss Partridge stopped by to give some final instructions before they set off. She basically repeated what Miss Vine had already told them about the route, advised them to warm up with some stretches, and told them that they could pace themselves and walk sections until they got their fitness up. "But the best thing for a stitch is to run through it." Off she went to her hockey girls.

Laura hung back to keep pace with Margery, who wasn't quite the worst. There were roughly three groups. At the front were relatively fit girls who were just useless at hockey. Then there were Laura and Margery and a few others. At the back came the fatties and the weedy girls who always tried to get out of everything due to their periods.

It was a cold day, and sharp on their lungs. One of the weedy girls had an asthma attack and dropped out. Margery and Laura gently jogged the first stretch and then started walking along the far end of the pitches, as Laura noticed that Margery was looking slightly puce. The path took them past a small house divided into two cottages. It was known as the "groundsman's cottages" even though a groundsman hadn't lived there for decades, as they were usually married and the one-bedroomed dwellings didn't suit a wife and family.

Instead, one cottage was generally taken by one of the teaching staff and the other by the summer tennis coach, lying empty the rest of the year.

"I heard Mr Rydell took the cottage this year, after Mr Carlisle left," they overheard another girl say to a friend as she jogged past and overtook them.

Laura suddenly felt as though her legs couldn't move. What if he was inside right now, and watching them? She had to literally count one-two, one-two in her head to keep herself moving. She hadn't even thought about where he might live. If she had done she would have presumed he would take a flat in town like most other teachers did. Cross country suddenly became a very different ordeal. She hoped desperately that they would vary the route in future weeks.

* * *

That night there was a surprise for them. Grace Grant called them into her office before prep and told them they would be getting a roommate. "Susie Clarke, a very nice girl. I hope you'll welcome her. She should be in similar sets to you. She's just come back from overseas which is why she's joining us late."

This was partly interesting, partly annoying. Charlotte went out on a limb. "Can we start prep late, so we can get to know her?"

The housemistress smiled. "Only if you can get everything done in a shorter time."

They raced up to the dorm to find a pretty, dark-haired girl unpacking her things.

"Hello, I'm Susie," she said. "Sorry to invade, I'm sure it's annoying for you."

They liked her instantly. "So you've just been abroad?" Laura asked. "Lucky you to miss the first week."

"In Italy. My great-grandmother's funeral. Don't worry," she said, seeing Laura's embarrassment. "Bisnonna was terribly old and had been ailing for years."

"So you're part Italian then?" asked Margery cautiously. "Do you speak it?" She didn't like the prospect of losing her unofficial crown of Modern Languages. Fortunately for Margery's reign, Susie confessed to understanding it and speaking it a bit but being hopeless at writing it. Languages really weren't her thing, she told them. She didn't say what was. Either way, Margery now felt comfortable enough to like Susie as much as the others had decided to.

"I guess the only question we really have for you then is Geography or German?" Charlotte said. Susie looked puzzled so Charlotte explained. "It's the main choice everyone has to make this year."

"Geography then, definitely not another language."

"I'm afraid you'll regret that bitterly," Charlotte said sadly.

Susie loved the diary idea and said she would join them. "I probably won't keep it up as being fickle is my worst vice, but let's see."

Eventually the others had to get to prep leaving Susie to her own devices.

* * *

"Dear Diary, you must be bored to death with me. I can't stop thinking about him. I'm sure he's sick of schoolgirl crushes by now. I think I should try a new focus. It's the Museum trip on Sunday, and the others plan to track down some Dunks guys."

8. Misbehaving

There was a buzz of excitement in chapel that Sunday among those who had convinced Mr Tyrrell to take them to Welchester Museum. He, poor man, was merely surprised and delighted by their sudden fervour for the Classics.

Laura's services were in big demand on the coach, as she carefully applied "art room eyeliner" and even rouge she had fashioned out of moisturiser and a filched oil pastel in Damask Rose. Susie, who had been allowed on the trip even though she didn't do Latin, had a smuggled lipstick she was happy to share.

"Ow! You jabbed my eye!" said Margery.

"I can't help it if there's potholes. Keep still."

They had discovered to their delight that Susie simply didn't do school rules. Morally or pragmatically, the new girl had no scruples whatsoever about breaking them.

She had already given the school food short shrift. "This is absolutely foul, I simply can't eat this. I'm Italian for God's sake." She was planning to have a cousin of hers, a medical student in Milan, send her a forged doctor's note in Italian excusing her from practically everything.

Sweet Miss Vine had fortunately been on their table the first day, and Susie had explained how it would simply be totally irresponsible of her to neglect her own health by making herself ill with ingredients proscribed by her doctor. Miss Vine was cowed by such eloquence, and Susie got her way.

They raced through the Museum as quickly as possible to maximise their time in the town. Any worries they had about how to approach the St Duncan's boys were taken care of by Susie. She simply walked up to a group of them and flashed a smile. Susie didn't know or care that they were actually Upper Sixth formers and prefects, and thus should have been far beyond their league.

"We've escaped prison for the day. Are there any pubs round here?"

Susie was pretty and charming enough to get away with murder, Laura thought. Instead of getting the brush off, they soon found themselves sitting around a café table with the premier league of St Duncan's boys. They felt slightly overawed - Margery in particular was very quiet and didn't dare speak - but Susie chatted away quite merrily.

A couple of the boys were particularly charismatic and good-looking and these two seemed most interested in Charlotte and Susie. Particularly after Susie managed to poke Charlotte in the back so she stuck her chest out in surprised reaction. Then there was a swotty looking boy, with a strong resemblance to Mr Poynter the History teacher, who ended up sitting by Margery.

A fourth boy, good looking but slightly quieter, seemed to be the most attentive to Laura but her thoughts wandered. She tried very hard to feel interested in them all but she couldn't stop comparing everyone to Mr Rydell. He was so much more mature and serious and worldly.

School dances were organised strictly by year, so there wasn't much hope of meeting these boys again at the Lower

School formal, but Susie was not daunted. She would always find a way if she felt strongly enough about something.

They all went for a walk around the church in the centre of town. There was only one reason to do this and it was to take advantage of the privacy that the ancient thick yew bushes afforded. Charlotte and Susie separated off with their respective boys, and Margery turned to go back to the museum. The swotty faced boy followed her, rather to her consternation. Laura couldn't help feeling that he looked like a pudding.

That left her with the quieter boy. "Shall we?" he said, rather awkwardly. They found a dark and undisturbed spot in the yews on the north of the graveyard, and he went to kiss her. She closed her eyes and tried to enjoy it, tried to wind the clock back to last summer when this would have been the greatest thrill ever, but all she could think of was Mr Rydell.

* * *

Their conquests were the talk of the coach on the way back. Getting off with an Upper Sixth boy was a huge feat for the Lower School, let alone a prefect. Susie held court with all the salacious details, which truth be told weren't many. But it was all in the telling.

Margery was at pains to point out that she had merely gone back to the Museum with her partner. "Margie, don't be square," Charlotte hissed at her.

"Well I don't think it's very nice kissing a boy five minutes after you meet them," Margery said indignantly. She was secretly annoyed - even though she didn't like to admit it even to herself - that her own partner hadn't displayed the courage or inclination to do so. She had never kissed a boy before.

Laura looked out of the windows, thinking. As the coach rolled back into the school she looked across at the cottages in the distance.

"You're looking very moony, Laura." Charlotte said. "Did you really like him?"

* * *

It was another hour until supper so Laura, tired of the endless boy talk, escaped with a book. She was tempted to go out of bounds just to get away from it all. She felt stifled.

The groundsman's cottages were drawing her with an invisible thread, so she deliberately found somewhere as far as possible in the opposite direction. This was a pavilion on the other side of the playing fields that was rarely used except in summer and was locked, but had two wooden benches outside. She sat on one of these.

She didn't know how long she had been reading, but it was quite a few chapters, when she sensed that someone was there. She looked up. It was him. Mr Rydell.

"Reading again?" He sat down beside her. "I'm not disturbing your peace?"

"No, not at all." What was he doing here? Why didn't he just greet her and walk on by?

"You weren't at lunch again." So he'd been looking for her? She explained about the Museum trip, for which they'd been given packed lunches. "I thought there were quite a few faces missing." So it wasn't just her, he had noticed others as well.

She wondered why he had stayed around for school lunch on Sunday. Most teachers went outside the school whenever they got the opportunity, if they weren't on duty. But then he was living on the premises, so perhaps that was the reason.

"Is the Museum worth a trip?" he asked.

"If you're Mr Tyrrell, yes. It's not bad really but we've all been so many times. I suppose I prefer seeing the actual places more," she added, not wanting to sound ungrateful.

"Are there many historic sites around here?"

"There's the remains of a Roman villa a bit further away. It has mosaics, exactly where they would have been all those thousands of years ago, where people actually walked on them."

"They don't seem real, do they, until you see things like that?" He understood. The Romans seemed so dead when they read about them in class, they may as well have never existed, been nothing but stories. Until you were actually faced with the physical traces their armies and colonists had left behind.

Both sat there silently for a while, looking across the fields. Laura's senses were heightened, she couldn't relax properly with him so near to her.

She went to clutch the edge of the bench with her hands, and accidentally put her hand on his in doing so. She hadn't realised it was there. "God, sorry!" She was mortified, withdrawing hers quickly. He must think she was trying to hold his hand.

"It's ok." He actually laughed, defusing the tension.

And then his face became serious again and they both looked at one another. It was longer than it should have been, unmistakably. Her stomach was flipping over again, but she couldn't dig her nails into her thumbs this time. She bit her lower lip instead, nervously.

Abruptly he stood up. "The bell will go soon, we should both make our way back."

* * *

"You're so dreamy Laura! Did you really like him that much?"

Laura started, then realised that Charlotte was talking about the St Duncan's boy. "He was very nice, but that's not what I was thinking about."

"Well what is it then? You've been on another planet all evening."

Across the room Susie was looking at her intently but didn't say anything. But at the first opportunity, when Margery and Charlotte had left the dorm, she slipped over to Laura's bed.

"It's another guy, isn't it?"

Laura said nothing. How could she?

"It's another guy, and for some reason you can't tell them. But if you need to talk, when you're ready, you can tell me. I won't judge."

Instinctively Laura knew that she wouldn't. Margery and Charlotte would have been agape and aghast, disapproving, disbelieving. She wasn't ready to talk to anyone yet - except her diary - but when she was, she realised it would be Susie whom she could confide in.

"Dear Diary, I don't think it's just in my head any more. But I'm not sure what I want or what I should do. I'm terrified, and miserable, and so, so happy."

9. Hot and cold

Susie Clarke sent Mr Peters into utter raptures from the first time he laid eyes on her. She was his ideal: young, very pretty, dark-eyed and dark-haired and extremely spirited. He discovered her full name was Susanna, and insisted on calling her it, drawing out the final two syllables in an affected way that he fancied sounded Italianate.

For her part, Susie could barely stop laughing at him. She picked him for a dirty old coot the moment she laid eyes on him. He wasn't the first man, nor would he be the last man, to letch over her like this.

Mr Peters had to contrive a way to get her inside his flat. It became his goal, his obsession. It never crossed his mind that his seduction attempts might fail. He started by offering Susie "catch up lessons" as she had missed so much of the previous year's syllabus, having studied quite different texts at her previous school.

This was rebuffed immediately. Susie knew she was bright and couldn't care less whether she passed her exams well or not. Even if she had wanted to excel at English, it wouldn't be by spending hours in a creepy teacher's stuffy flat.

Miss Wingrove had also been made aware of the Head of Department's proclivities and was keeping her eyes open as Mrs Grayson had hoped. She had actually frustrated a couple of Mr Peters' attempts to single Susie out of her own classes. He had appeared at the door, and asked if she "could possibly spare Susanna Clarke for a moment."

"Is it very urgent, Mr Peters?"

"It's merely that I have the list of reading she needs to catch up on," he explained in a silken tone.

"In that case I'll make sure we finish on time, and Susie can join you immediately break starts."

Susie then showed up shoulder to shoulder with Laura and Charlotte as bodyguards, and Mr Peters was forced to hand the list over without paying her any further personal attentions.

He tried once more with a similar excuse, but was again foiled by Miss Wingrove. "Given the amount of syllabus Susie has missed, I think it would be helpful for her to have her full attendance in my class, Mr Peters."

No further attempts were made. He needed a new strategy.

* * *

German was becoming simultaneously a dread and a desperate joy for Laura. She dreaded it in case Mr Rydell didn't look at her or didn't speak to her, and was filled with wild joy when he did. Every lesson was an ordeal, the tension she felt in his presence wound up by the exhilaration.

Something, at some point, had to give. She knew that, she just didn't know what or when.

At times he seemed almost cold and indifferent to her, and her heart crashed in a thousand shards every time, then surged when he did address her directly.

No one else was aware that anything was going on, not even Margery despite her earlier observations. Had Susie been in their German class it might have been different. She was very astute about this kind of thing. Laura had wavered over confiding in her several times but always held back. She feared it would break the spell to actually put it into words, to confess it.

Largely thanks to Susie's prominent presence, the others remarked less on Laura's changed character. She was much quieter these days and much more absorbed in her own thoughts. But she couldn't concentrate on things in the same way she had previously.

Every time she went to read somewhere she hoped he might show up, but he never did. He occasionally nodded to her if he saw her outside the German class, such as at meal times, but beyond that she feared he was avoiding her.

And yet there were still moments in class where they caught one another's eye, just a fraction of a second too long.

* * *

Charlotte had her own problems. She faced a venomous fight to hold onto her coveted position as right wing in the hockey team. Though Charlotte was by far the best candidate, Teresa Hubert had been sucking up to Miss Partridge all term and playing as dirty as she could to spoil Charlotte's game whenever she could get away with it.

Why Miss Partridge would be taken in by Teresa remained a mystery to Charlotte, unless she fancied her or something. It was generally accepted that any games mistress must be a lesbian, and they had always suspected Miss Partridge of having a particularly close friendship with Miss Vine. No one really minded though, because they all liked Miss Vine, or rather felt slightly sorry for her.

"This place really seethes with sex and intrigue, doesn't it?" Charlotte remarked one day to Susie.

"Naturally it does. What else would you expect with several hundred girls on the cusp of womanhood, and a load of hopeless old sticks suppressing their urges for decade after decade?"

Susie's take on everything was quite different to theirs. They had been particularly shocked - and fascinated - to discover that Susie wasn't a virgin. It was highly unusual for anyone in the Lower School to have "gone all the way". Some of the Sixth Form girls came back after each summer break on the Pill, claiming their doctor had prescribed it for acne, but everyone knew better.

The three others had grilled Susie endlessly about what sex was like and she had been quite frank and descriptive, but there was a basic gulf between her experiences and theirs that made certain things hard to translate. Margery in particular was very shockable about such matters which restricted discussion.

Laura had never thought much about losing her virginity before, she had assumed it would probably all happen at university. But now Mr Rydell was in her thoughts she found herself wondering what it would be like with him. Masterful, she thought, not fumbling like a St Duncan's boy.

The boy she'd kissed on the Latin trip had written to her a couple of times, and she had sent polite but essentially platonic notes back. It was enough to just officially have a boyfriend, you didn't actually have to see them or do anything with them. Simply that they existed at all and wrote to you was sufficient for social cachet.

* * *

A couple of times a term the school had an exeat, when pupils were allowed to go home for the weekend. If your parents lived too far away you were usually assigned a guardian in the town. This was the situation for Laura, who was officially the term-time ward of a nice couple in their early sixties who acted as guardian for several Francis Hall girls. She actually rarely saw them as she usually went to stay with Margery instead.

Susie had an aunt and uncle who lived near enough to act as guardians as her parents lived further away and frequently travelled overseas. Margery had offered to invite her along with Laura, but Susie had other plans.

"I'm going to spend the weekend at St Duncan's," she said. "It's all planned. I'll kip in Julian and Darius's dorm, no funny business, just for a lark. If a master comes by they'll hide me in the cupboard. Apparently it's very spacious inside."

This shocking news led to a flurry of questioning as to how Susie planned to get there and slip inside without anyone noticing. But this had all been carefully thought out as well. They were as impressed as they were anxious for her.

"You would definitely, definitely get expelled for that," Margery warned. "The boys too."

"I'd better not get caught then!" Susie laughed. It was amazing how she truly didn't care, she felt absolutely none of the fears that constrained the other three on a daily basis.

"But what if you do? It's not just about you, it's their A-level year, it would ruin everything."

"Julian is St Duncan's rugby captain. Darius's father is as rich as Croesus. Trust me, they won't be expelled. I'd be surprised if they were even gated for more than a week."

Margery remained upset, but Susie was undaunted.

I wonder how Susie would handle Mr Rydell if she were me, Laura thought. Would she simply go up to him and make the first move like she did with the St Duncan's boys?

And when she thought this, she realised that this was exactly what she was waiting for. For one of them - for him - to finally make a move.

* * *

Margery was the least happy member of the dorm that term. Charlotte and Susie had become so intensely chummy, and Laura so self-absorbed, that she was feeling left out. The swotty looking boy hadn't written to her which had privately devastated her. It didn't help that the others continually referred to him as "the Pudding".

He was the first boy who had ever shown interest in her, or at least she had thought he had, and it hadn't gone further than looking at some museum exhibits together.

So Margery threw herself into her schoolwork as usual, burying herself in prep, keeping up her record of straight As. None of them noticed that she was unhappy. Her diary was her primary confidant, as it was for Laura.

"Dear Diary, I miss him when I don't see him, and I miss him when we don't speak. For the first time I understand that verse in Song of Songs - that thou wert as my brother - just to be with him, anyhow, would be enough. Everything feels as though it's growing darker."

10. Crossing the line

Laura was running another errand, delivering a pile of photocopied forms on behalf of the school secretary. She had been passing by the staffroom after the last lesson of the day and been commandeered.

The empty English classrooms seemed eerie at this hour. It was still light, but starting to fade. She hurried through them, and finished with the modern languages block: first French, then German.

She honestly wasn't expecting Mr Rydell to still be in his classroom. She had assumed he was in the staffroom, amid the clink of teacups and conversation that always emanated from that mysterious sanctum.

About to walk in and drop off the last papers, she stopped dead when she saw him by his desk.

"I had to deliver these," she said.

"Come in." He was cleaning something off the blackboard.

She entered, walking past him to put the forms on his desk. As she turned to go he looked at her and she stopped, looking back up at him, and they both stood there.

Moments passed. Too long to ignore. She could not speak.

Teachers and pupils do not stand gazing into each other's eyes, in silence. Not like this. She was half his age. But the line was already crossed.

He took a step towards her. His hair fell over his forehead, his eyes dark grey, chiselled features tense.

"I've been fighting this for so long."

A muscle twitched as he clenched his jaw. He was looking at her, serious, no joy in his expression. His eyes seemed almost sad.

Her stomach was lurching. It was the moment she had longed for, dreamed about, and yet it felt more like a terrible taboo than ecstasy.

He stroked his hand down the side of her face, moving her hair back.

"This is something that could ruin both our lives," he said.

She couldn't speak. She wanted to tell him that she didn't care, that she only wanted to live for the moment. But she was terrified.

"Wanting you this much... it makes me willing to risk everything."

His lips came down on hers, warm and firm, and her first sensation was relief. At last! Then joy, and terror, and desire. His tongue invaded her mouth, exploring her, tasting her. It was a union: so different from French kissing the St Duncan's boy, or the boy from her holiday.

She was in his arms, and he was holding her gently at first, then more strongly, pressing her harder against him as his own desire for her grew.

Her head was spinning, racing. There were two of her: a wild, abandoned purely physical Laura who wanted and needed him as though she was drinking him in. Her hands felt his body, his warmth, the firmness of his muscles, the flat, hard planes of his chest through his shirt.

Then there was a panicking, mind-whirling, Laura-of-thoughts with a thousand questions and doubts and anxieties. What if someone came in? What if someone saw them?

Then he turned her so her back was against the wall and pushed her hard up against it, his passion increasing. He crushed his body against hers, bruising her lips as he kissed her. She felt as though he was devouring her.

His hand moved over her breast, feeling it through the thin wool of her school jumper, making her body arch and press towards his. His lips were on her neck, he twisted his fingers through her hair to draw her closer to him.

His left hand should be under my head, and his right hand should embrace me...

And then he broke away. Ran a hand through his own hair, moved away. "God, this is madness." He was speaking to himself.

She was left breathless, torn away.

He regained some composure. "You must go. This is completely wrong."

Overwhelmed, she fled.

* * *

The coldness of the evening air revived her enough to straighten out her appearance in the nearest cloakroom before going into prep. Thank God there was no one else around. Her hair was everywhere, falling around her face. Her clothes were rumpled and coming apart. Her lips were bruised and swollen.

Shock put her into survival mode. She tucked her blouse back in. Splashed her face with water and dried it. Smoothed and tied back her hair.

Then she leant on the basin and hung her head, closing her eyes for a few seconds.

Everything throbbed.

Like an automaton, she rushed to get her books and to join the others before the second bell went. Would they notice anything amiss? She felt like she was naked, that the whole world must be looking at her and knowing. She felt that there was writing all over her, that everyone would be staring. She held her head low, tried to hide in the crowd, sat down and huddled herself over her work.

A sharp nudge. WHAT'S WRONG??? Charlotte was looking at her, concerned.

ALL FINE she scribbled back, erasing it almost immediately. She wasn't fine. She would never be fine again.

* * *

Somehow she found a still place inside her. It enabled her to get through supper, go through the motions of conversation, walk back with the others, use the bathroom, get ready for bed.

"I'm so bored of me," she told Charlotte. "Tell me an exciting story about your life."

Charlotte launched into a tirade about Teresa Hubert and Miss Partridge.

In one evening she had learned to act. To dissemble. To stash real-Laura deep away, in the still place.

She suspected that Susie was not convinced, but she didn't care. She dreaded her dreams tonight, she knew they would be confused, and she feared she would talk in her sleep.

What was going to happen in their next German class? How could she face him? Did he hate her now? Had she ruined his life?

Would she ever feel like that again, be in his arms again?

And she wondered what he was doing now. Her mind reached out across the dark playing fields, to where the groundsman's cottages were. He would be alone, she thought. She feared he was angry. She missed him.

"Dear Diary, everything has gone wrong."

* * *

As it was, sleep evaded her. She lay for what seemed like hours, hearing the others breathe, Margery snoring slightly. Her pillow seemed alternately too hot or icy cold when she turned it. Her mind kept racing, she felt alternately excited and worried.

In the end she got up and crept to the bathroom. She sat on the cold tiles, her arms wrapped around her legs.

Then someone came in. It was Susie. "Come with me." Susie led her to the fire escape - it was strictly forbidden to go out on it, but had to be left accessible nonetheless. Occasionally people sneaked out on it to smoke.

The night air was freezing by then, there would be an early frost tonight. It made the stars brighter.

"I like it here," Susie said. She kept her voice low. There weren't any teachers' windows nearby, but it always paid to be careful. "I often come here while you guys are sleeping. I can't sleep as early as lights out."

The fire escape was on the side of the building, so there were no panoramic views of the playing fields, but you could see about half of them. Not as far as the cottages, but Laura had looked through the dorm windows at them beforehand. No light had been on.

"So what's happening?" Susie said. "Is it Jonathan?"

"Who?" Laura was momentarily thrown.

"Obviously not then. Jonathan - your supposed boyfriend from St Duncan's."

He always signed his letters Jon. But even if he hadn't he seemed so remote, so long ago now, that she would have forgotten anyway.

"So is it a girl then? As I said I won't judge. My cousin's gay." Susie couldn't see how it could be another boy, Laura had never mentioned anyone else, and there were no boys anywhere around that she could think of. There was a younger lad who helped the old gardener but he was simple.

"It's Mr Rydell."

When she spoke his name, it was as though the whole night sky rang with it. It pealed across the playing fields, she was sure he must hear it. All the world was echoing with it.

Susie wasn't unduly shocked. "You have a crush on Mr Rydell? He's very good looking, I can't blame your taste. Or has he been mean to you or something?"

Mean? Laura couldn't imagine him ever being mean. He was the absolute inverse.

"It's not... a crush as such," she said.

Susie waited. The words were on Laura's lips but she struggled to say them. Would Susie believe her? Would she think it was wrong or stupid?

"I was in his classroom earlier, and..." It was so hard to articulate. Putting it into words, the enormity of what had happened.

"And?"

"We kissed."

"Christ!"

Susie was silent for a moment, absorbing the news, and Laura dug her nails into her thumbs.

"I take it that this was ok? I mean he didn't force himself on you?"

God no. How could he? Laura started to explain. Briefly, without too much detail. How he looked at her. How he had sat and spoken with her several times. How it had just happened in the German classroom. How he had suddenly told her to leave.

Then it was all too much, the brief exhilaration and the fear and the anxiety, and the isolation she felt. Bottling up how she felt about him for weeks had been hard enough. Then today, and having to keep it from everyone. And not knowing where she stood now, what he felt, what she could expect next time she saw him. Now it was all out and she couldn't stop the tears.

Susie put her arms around Laura and hugged her. "It's going to be ok. It'll work out."

11. On edge

Laura couldn't touch breakfast the next morning. The others noticed her loss of appetite and how pale and tired she looked. She had barely eaten anything the evening before so she was able to attribute it to still being unwell. Susie cast her a sympathetic look but kept her confidence.

It was two more days until Monday and the next German lesson. She had the whole weekend to wonder if she would bump into Mr Rydell. But she felt deep down that he would avoid her.

It was torment. Everywhere she went she found herself surreptitiously looking out for him. Wondering, hoping beyond hope, that he would appear.

Concentrating on Saturday morning lessons was hard enough at the best of times because the weekend had pretty much arrived, and everyone was longing for lunch after which they would finally be at leisure. Hockey teams would play home matches or be driven off in the school coach to play away games but everyone else could do what they wanted.

This particular morning was agony. Laura could only stare at the clock, wondering if she might see him between lessons, or after lunch.

She would have liked to spend some time with Susie but unfortunately Susie had detention.

"Let's talk later this afternoon," she told Laura at lunch. "I'm in the clink for Geography yet again, but they'll surely let us out before nightfall."

* * *

In the history of Francis Hall there had never been hostilities as venomous as those that had broken out between Mrs Ayers and Susie Clarke.

It was Mrs Ayers' fault for starting it. She had been in a particularly foul mood the first time Susie came into her Geography lesson, and attempted to give the girl a demerit for not having the right textbook. When Susie quite rightfully and politely pointed out that it was her first day and no one had given her any books yet, Mrs Ayers shrieked at her for answering back and tried to give her a detention as well.

Most girls would have backed down, but Susie did not. The matter escalated to Mrs Grayson, who was forced to find a resolution that was fair to Susie without enraging Mrs Ayers. There was no way to do this without revoking the demerit and the detention, effectively meaning that Susie had won. No amount of Mrs Grayson phrasing it as an "unfortunate misunderstanding" could save Mrs Ayers' humiliation. She had never lost before.

From that moment Mrs Ayers hated Susie with every fibre of her being and poured forth the full force of her venom upon her. As a result, Susie decided that Mrs Ayers would have to be destroyed for once and for all, but knew she was going to have to play a very long game to achieve this. The alleged blood of Machiavelli didn't run in her family's veins for nothing, so she was prepared to take her time.

To start her campaign, Susie became perhaps the most exceptional student of Geography that Francis Hall had ever witnessed. She was a bright girl, and it didn't take much more than a bit of extra study to excel in a subject like Geography. The hours spent in the library poring over the names of cloud formations and trying to memorise the rivers in Africa she considered to be the equivalent to equipping a suit of armour. Putting in extra hours on her homework was loading her gun.

"Mrs Ayers really has it in for you doesn't she?" someone commented, when Susie's latest, flawless essay was given a C.

Susie made it as difficult as possible for Mrs Ayers to give her demerits and detentions. She was always on time, her hair and clothes were immaculate beyond measure. She was a neat girl anyway so this wasn't hard.

Despite this, Mrs Ayers continued to hand out punishments for the slightest, most spurious reason. Susie never complained. She simply used the detentions to study even harder at Geography. Her zeal mystified the others, who couldn't see why anyone would put in so much effort for The Axe.

"It's necessary," was all Susie said.

But Mrs Ayers alone knew that Susie had not submitted to her. So while she continued to hate and punish her, she began slightly to fear her.

Margery queried the endless detentions, but Susie just replied "give her enough rope."

* * *

Laura remained nauseous with misery and anxiety all day. It was miserable weather too, rainy with a blustering autumn wind, and the pitches got so waterlogged that matches were cancelled.

The only thing keeping everyone going was the thought of next weekend's exeat. "Five more days," Charlotte counted. They were hanging out in the dorm because Teresa Hubert and her group had already claimed the common room. It simply wasn't big enough for all of them.

A major task on the exeat weekend for many girls was to come back with an outfit for the half term dance. The Lower School formal was held the day before the Upper School event, but was considered no less important to those attending.

There were strict rules for outfits: skirts still below the knee, modest necklines, nothing too tight or clingy. Any girl wearing clothes considered unsuitable was required to change into her gym kit or return to her house. This was tantamount to the same thing, since no one could countenance appearing before the St Duncan's boys in a tracksuit.

For Margery the entire affair was an ordeal as she was shy about her appearance. She also still had the wardrobe of a young girl, no one had realised that she was growing up and might need something more sophisticated. Most of the other girls planned to wear actual cocktail dresses, even off-the-shoulder. To get away with this usually required a last-minute hasty rearrangement of taffeta sleeves, once safely through the dress inspection.

Margery didn't want to be the only girl there wearing a knee-length rah-rah skirt and baggy cardigan.

"We'll go shopping on the exeat," Laura promised her.

Margery doubted her local village shops would have anything. Maybe she could persuade her father to drive them into the town.

Laura was looking forward to staying with Margery, but now she couldn't think past this weekend: spending two entire days with minimal chance of seeing Mr Rydell.

Susie returned back from her scheduled hours of punishment. Fortunately it had been Mr Tyrrell rostered on to monitor the miscreants this weekend, and he barely noticed what anyone did. Which in Susie's case was reading a forbidden novel masked with the dust jacket of a school library book.

"You're not still going through with your plan, are you, Susie?" Margery said. She still couldn't believe that Susie would actually dare to spend an entire weekend hidden in Darius's and Julian's dormitory at St Duncan's. It was an absolutely mad scheme.

"Of course. I could hardly cancel now, they're expecting me."

* * *

Susie and Laura eventually found some time to talk alone in the music building. They were fed up with being cooped up at Michaelmas House, so early on Saturday evening they braved the foul weather and made their way there.

The practice rooms were usually occupied at the weekend, but they rightly guessed that even the keenest musicians would be reluctant to go out in the current downpour. All four boarding houses were a long walk away from the music building.

Inside they had their pick of empty rooms. Laura sat on a piano stool, and Susie pushed some sheet music out of the way and perched on the table, swinging her legs.

"Monday then," Susie said. "The big showdown with the handsome Mr Rydell."

Laura felt embarrassed. "Nothing's going to happen in front of everyone. He'll probably just ignore me and try to pretend it never happened."

"I don't think he'll leave it at that. It wouldn't be safe, just to assume you'd drop it as well. Plus there's the fact that he likes you strongly enough to have crossed the line in the first place. It's not like it was just a peck on the lips, it all sounded pretty full on from what you said. I suspect he's wrestling with his conscience."

"What would you do?" Laura asked. "I mean if he just says nothing and that's it. Or says it's a bad idea."

"If I were you? If I really liked him, really and truly and utterly, I wouldn't take no for an answer."

How did one "not take no for an answer"? What did it even mean?

"Do you think he's worried about the age gap?"

"Undoubtedly. But I shouldn't let it worry you. Bisnonna was only fourteen when she married my great-grandfather, and he was nearly thirty," Susie told her. "And Juliet, and the Virgin Mary."

All these examples seemed so remote, lost in time and history. Laura couldn't feel a connection to them.

"Dear Diary, I'm so nervous about Monday I feel sick. Susie is the only person I can talk to. I just have to get this over with. I don't even know what I want. I need to think like Susie, not like me."

12. Making a choice

Laura could hardly breathe during the next German lesson. She was on edge the entire time, wanting to avoid looking at Mr Rydell but not being able to stop. He had them write out exercises, and spent much of the class marking work. He rarely looked up.

The lesson went agonisingly slowly. She didn't know if she was more terrified that he might just try to pretend it never happened, or if he confronted her about it. Would he be angry?

She studied him at his desk. His eyes were fixed on the books he was correcting, his face set and resolute. Look at me, she willed. Please look at me and give me some kind of sign. At least let me know you don't hate me.

Trying to concentrate on her own work was very hard. But she didn't want to mess it up in case it looked like she was deliberately trying to give him cause to detain her. That was Teresa Hubert's pathetic trick. Laura wanted him to approach her on his own terms.

When the bell went everyone else scrambled to leave, since it was break time. She picked up her things more reluctantly.

"Cathy, Laura, could you both stay behind for a moment."

This was it.

Mr Rydell deliberately didn't even look at her as he gave the order. Her stomach was churning worse than she could remember.

He also looked more devastating to her than he ever had before, serious and commanding. His lips were set in a firm line. He also seemed taller than ever, so much older than her. What was she even thinking that he might be seriously interested in someone like her, just a schoolgirl?

He dealt with Cathy first. She had missed classes through illness, and he was setting her the work she needed to do to catch up. It only took a couple of minutes, and then she scuttled away.

Now it was just the two of them. Laura was so nervous she felt nauseous. He began. He spoke looking directly at her and yet even though he met her eyes it felt like he was speaking from behind a screen.

"I would like to apologise to you for what happened the other day. It was completely unacceptable of me. I won't try to make excuses, but I can promise you it will never happen again."

She said nothing, only looked back at him. At his eyes, the faint shadows she also saw around them. He had lost sleep too.

"This won't make any difference to how I treat you in class. It was entirely my fault," he continued.

It sounded rehearsed. He was saying what he knew he had to say, not what he wanted to say. It gave her courage.

What would Susie do?

Don't take no for an answer.

Still without speaking, Laura went up to him. She put her hands on either side of his face, and pulled him down to kiss her. He didn't have time to react, to step back.

As soon as her lips were on his he closed his eyes, and he groaned as the kiss deepened. "Laura…" he said, the start of a protest, but his arms went around her and she clung to him.

It was insanity. Anyone could have walked past.

She felt the heat of him again, tasted him. She wanted to drown in him. He returned the kiss in full measure.

"It wasn't just you," she said as she broke away.

He sat on the edge of the desk, and looked directly at her. She remained standing, and their eyes were at the same level.

"Is this what you want?" he asked.

For a second she was terrified, but there was only one answer. She could barely whisper.

"Yes."

"I'm not a schoolboy, Laura. I can't have a relationship with you on those terms. It's all or nothing."

He was trying to scare her, to put her off. He wanted her to be the one to decide against this, to run away.

To spare them both.

But the sight of him, the smell of his skin, the thought of his hands on her, the thought of just being with him overtook her.

"It's still yes."

He stood and brought her to him again, kissing her more tenderly this time. It was gentle, exploring her, his tongue intertwining with hers, promising what was to come.

Then he broke off and became more businesslike. "Where are you going for exeat this weekend?"

"To Margery's."

"Can you cancel? Come and stay with me. When everyone's leaving, come to the cottage. I'll be there before you as I don't have a class at the end of the day."

What was she going to tell Margery?

"Okay."

"If you can't manage it or you change your mind it's okay. Just let me know."

"I won't change my mind."

* * *

The rest of the week passed agonisingly slowly, in a different kind of limbo. Laura was carrying this huge secret but she had to sit through German classes with him as normal. A couple of times when he glanced at her she thought she saw a question in his eyes. He was uncertain as well. They were both getting into something unknown.

Margery was very disappointed when Laura withdrew from their plans. Laura managed to imply, without actually stating it, that she was instead going to stay with Mr and Mrs Jones, the guardian couple in town.

"I can't think why you want to visit them all of a sudden. Yes I do. It's a boy, isn't it?"

Laura felt ashamed for deceiving Margery. "Sort of."

"It either is or it isn't. It's that boy from St Duncan's, the one you write to. I hope he's worth it." Margery was still bitter over the Pudding.

"I really am sorry Margery. I can't fully explain."

"What you mean is that you don't think I'll understand."

Laura vowed to herself that she would tell Margery eventually. She hated keeping secrets this important from her friends. But she had no choice. The risk one was thing. But her own conflicted emotions also held her back. Until she had figured out her own feelings she couldn't bring herself to tell them.

* * *

Teresa Hubert, who always had an eye for stirring the pot, noticed that Margery was glum and withdrawn. She didn't care for Margery at all but thought there might be advantage in extending friendship.

Margery was not quite so easily won. Teresa had been spiteful towards her since the fourth form so she didn't trust her at all.

Sidling up to her between classes one morning Teresa tried to open a conversation. "What are you doing for exeat? Did you invite Laura again?"

It wasn't any of Teresa's business but Margery was piqued by Laura's change of plans. "No, she had to stay with her town guardians."

"How odd," said Teresa, scenting opportunity. "She always stays with you, doesn't she?"

Margery knew when Teresa was digging and didn't rise to the bait. Even if Laura had flaked out on her she was still her friend.

"What are you wearing to the formal?" Teresa asked, changing the subject. She strongly suspected that Margery wouldn't have anything appropriate. Whenever they were in mufti - out of school uniform - Margery always looked very frumpy.

"I haven't decided yet."

"I expect that Susie Clarke will wear something tarty. She's quite a slag, isn't she?"

Margery was not yet loyal enough to Susie to defend her to the fullest, particularly as she had felt shut out by her friendship with Charlotte. And recently she seemed as thick as thieves with Laura.

"I really wouldn't know," she said, not taking a position.

Teresa smiled nastily, and left.

* * *

Charlotte was starting to excel at hockey. Something had clicked with her, mentally and physically, and she had gone from being a good player to exceptional.

Unbeknownst to Miss Partridge it was Charlotte's dalliance with the St Duncan's boys that had triggered the change. Julian, the boy who had flirted with her, was the school rugby captain. He had even written to her a couple of times which had been flattering though she suspected she wasn't the only iron in his fire.

Charlotte was naturally competitive. Julian's attention not only gave her confidence but it made her want to match his success.

It was a wild dream for a Lower School girl to make the First Eleven hockey team though it had been achieved in the past. And the Seconds were certainly achievable even if the current team was composed entirely of sixth formers.

Charlotte knew fewer girls liked to play on the left wing so she yielded her coveted place as right wing to Teresa Hubert and started playing on the left whenever she could. She found it harder in some ways but it also gave her a better tactical perspective.

"What's come over you? You're like a machine," one of the other girls complained, struggling to keep up with her in drills.

Charlotte had also worked on becoming fitter and faster. There were a couple of sixth form girls who did competitive cross country and trained in their spare time, so she joined them. They were hearty girls who didn't mind if they were running with a Lower School girl so long as she didn't hold them back.

It didn't take long before her hockey game began to transform. Miss Partridge had no idea what was behind Charlotte's quantum leap in progress but she did start to think about trying her out for the senior squad.

* * *

Laura had decided to tell Susie about the plan to stay with Mr Rydell over exeat. She felt like she would burst if she didn't confide in someone. She also needed reassurance or some kind of reaction since her own feelings were so confused.

Susie was delighted when Laura revealed her secret. "A dirty weekend with a teacher!" she said. "It makes my trip to St Duncan's seem very tame."

Laura wanted to protest about it being called a dirty weekend but in reality she had a creeping fear inside. How far would Mr Rydell expect her to go? She remembered what he had said about "all or nothing". At the time she had been certain she wanted all, or could cope with all, but now she faltered.

Noticing the worry in her eyes, Susie was perceptive enough to guess what it was about. "If you're not ready, you just tell him," she said. "Just because you stay over doesn't mean you have to go all the way. You're not on the Pill are you?" Laura wasn't. "Well make sure you tell him that too. You don't want to end up like that girl everyone always goes on about."

"Lucy Martin."

"Yes, her."

Laura wondered what Lucy Martin was doing now. Had she ever made it to university? She must be in her early twenties now, it seemed ancient. Then she remembered that Mr Rydell was even older than that. When she was with him his age never mattered to her. If anything it was a thrill that he was so much older and more experienced than her.

But now she thought about Lucy Martin, and felt anxious. Was she out of her depth?

"Don't worry about it, I'm sure he won't let that happen," Susie said. "You'd have more fear of that with a Dunks boy not knowing what to do."

"You'd better be careful yourself then," Laura said, referring to Susie's own plans to spend the weekend with Darius.

"Like I said, it's solely for fun. We're not planning an orgy."

* * *

"Dear Diary, I don't know if it's safe to write my thoughts here any longer. I want to write more than ever but I find it harder and harder to write anything. And it's not just about me anymore, is it?"

PART II

Falling

We that were friends to-night have found
A sudden fear, a secret flame:
I am on fire with that soft sound
You make, in uttering my name.

James Elroy Flecker

13. Losing control

It was Friday evening and the day was drawing to a close. There was a whirl of activity as girls rushed off to be picked up by parents and guardians for the exeat. Some had to wait until Saturday morning if their parents lived further away, but school formalities were relaxed and there was a spirit of holidays.

Laura felt strangely left out. She wasn't sure why. She couldn't wait to see Mr Rydell though she felt nearly sick with terror. It felt like an invisible curtain was coming down between her and everyone else, that she was moving to a place they couldn't visit.

Making her way up the path towards the groundsman's cottages was like walking the gauntlet. She had chosen a good moment to slip away, but it still felt as though a thousand eyes were upon her. It would only take one person to spot her and investigate and everything would be a disaster.

But somehow, she made it.

She knocked and he opened the door and she stepped inside. She had never been in the cottages before. The interior was quite spartan, much like their dorms. The school had apparently used similar fittings.

It was strange to see Mr Rydell in casual clothes. Male staff at Francis Hall were required to wear a jacket and tie. Seeing him wearing something else was strange. It was like discovering another person: he had this whole other life that she knew nothing about.

"I'm glad you made it," he said. Then his arms were around her, and they were kissing, urgently. It was a relief as much as it was wonderful. It took some of the strangeness away.

Laura still had her thick school coat on, restricting her. He slipped his hands inside it and pulled it down off her shoulders to the floor.

Now she was free to wrap her arms around him equally, as he again pushed her against the wall. He moved his thigh up between hers, hard, and she nearly lost her balance.

She was pinned, she couldn't move except to kiss him back and let him kiss her face, her neck, run his hands over her body.

When he broke away his voice was ragged. "Christ, what you do to me. I fully intended to start by offering you a drink and just talking, but something overtakes me."

She was breathless as well. Scared by the force of his passion and her own, and his strength and the control he had over her, but also thrilled by the way she was able to affect him.

"What would you like? Wine? Coke? Tea?"

She didn't want tea because of the time it took to make it. She didn't much like wine, but it might calm her nerves. Or she might drink too quickly and be ill. Coke seemed like the childish option.

"Just water if you have it."

He fetched her a glass, and they sat down on the sofa. The gas fire was identical to other ones in the school. It was disconcerting to have all these reminders.

"This isn't something I've ever done before," he said. "Crossing the line with a pupil is the most serious thing any teacher can do. I don't know what is different about you, but from the first time I saw you I haven't been able to get you out of my head."

Laura could hardly speak. She managed to say "likewise".

They were sitting apart, not touching, and she didn't know what to do with herself except hold the glass of water.

"Come here." He took the water out of her hand and pulled her closer to him, his arm around her.

"You have no idea of the times I've seen you and had to walk away, because I feared I would do something that I would regret."

"I used to love it when you came and talked to me," she said.

He gave her one of his rare smiles. "Now at least we can do that without fear of the bell."

He asked about her time at Francis Hall, her parents, what she liked and what she didn't like. And he told her about his life, what he'd done at university, his previous jobs, his plans for the future. She was very comfortable now, resting against his side, the warmth of him next to her.

It felt that they talked for hours, Laura lost track of the time. She was amazed how well they got on, how easy it was. Even despite the differences in age and experience they were on some same, shared level. Occasionally she worried about sounding childish but mainly it was fine. She felt, as she had felt the times before when he talked to her, that they were like co-conspirators. It was the two of them against school, against the world. They laughed at the same things, admired the same things.

It was the little things he noticed about her that amazed her. He remembered the books he had seen her reading, even trivial things she had said. He was genuinely interested in her.

Then he noticed it was getting late. "You must be starving." Laura realised she was. She had totally lost her appetite the past week and barely been able to eat a thing earlier in the day.

"My plans were to cook for you and take you to bed, but I'm running behind schedule," he said.

Her stomach flipped. He noticed the apprehension in her eyes, and sought to reassure her. "I know what I said the other day, but there's no pressure. Just being with you and holding you is enough."

They ate, and then he led her up the narrow stairs to the cottage's small bedroom. It had a double bed at least.

Afterwards when the others asked she could never remember how she took her clothes off, it was a blur. She did remember that he unbuttoned her blouse, unhooked her bra, slipped her underwear down.

"I want to see you naked, completely mine."

Mine. It was the first time he had said anything possessive towards her. Although she felt like they were on the same team, the two of them, it had never been expressed. She didn't know what she was to him. It felt absurd to use a word like "boyfriend" that got used for St Duncan's boys and the tame, pen-pal relationships they had.

Laura felt shy but also strangely proud as he uncovered her. She was amazed that she affected him so much, her body arousing the desire that she saw in his eyes. He took her to the bed. His hands were warm on her skin, and she wanted him to run them over her body but didn't know how to ask.

He threw his own clothes off quickly, and lay next to her, resting on one elbow. His chest was so broad and strong, he looked so powerful. She loved it as much as it made her nervous.

He kissed her. "You're still a virgin, aren't you?"

She nodded.

"I want you very badly but if it's too much we can hold off. Just let me know and I'll stop."

She wasn't sure what she wanted yet. She wanted him as close to her as possible but she didn't know if it would hurt or if she was ready.

He caressed her body, moving his hand over her left breast, playing with her nipple. No one had done this to her before. It felt unbelievably sensitive under his fingers as he teased it to hardness, and then brought his mouth down upon it.

Laura gasped and felt her back arch towards him. It made her throb down below. She ran her hands through his hair, as he swirled his tongue around her swollen nipple. His hands caressed her waist, her stomach, moving lower to her thighs.

Then suddenly she felt his hand move toward her inner thighs. She froze momentarily, then he slid his fingers between her folds, brushing her clitoris. No one had ever touched her there before.

It was electric, she felt a sharp pang in her groin that shot up to her stomach. Instinctively she moaned and pushed towards his hand. His fingers were firm and knew exactly where to apply pressure.

He raised his head from her breast. "You're very wet."

Laura wasn't sure if this was good or not but he smiled so she figured it must be.

She had a brief flashback to class and the image of him standing at the blackboard, instructing them. Mr Rydell, their teacher. And now he was touching her in the most intimate places and in the most intimate way, with something of the same decisiveness and authority. He was instructing her, instructing her body.

He took her hand and moved it onto him. She had no idea how warm and hard he would feel, nothing they'd learnt in Biology or speculated about in the dorm had prepared her for this. Her fingers could barely wrap around it. She couldn't imagine there was any way they could actually do it.

But he shifted up so he was leaning over her, and pushed her thighs apart with his knees.

His eyes were dark with desire. He had promised her he would stop, but he clearly wanted this. The thought flashed through her mind that he might not stop even if she did resist.

She felt him pressing against her opening, her wetness helping him in. It hurt - he was so large - and she bit her lip to stop herself crying out. She tried to shift back to ease the pressure but his hands were gripping her hips and holding her against him, not letting her get away.

"I want to be your first," he said, looking deep into her eyes.

He pushed into her and the pain increased, and yet she wanted it. She wanted to do this. She wanted him closer to her, as close as possible, for him to take possession of her. He withdrew a little and she relaxed, closed her eyes, and then he pressed into her again.

At some point there was a particularly sharp pain, and around this time his lips were on hers before she could cry out, and then against her neck, and he was saying her name.

Then holding her tightly, almost crushing her as his hard, muscular chest pressed against her breasts, he thrust forward and they were finally joined. She was sore and it throbbed but he was with her, in her, fully.

He waited for a few moments, holding her still, until he felt her relax. Then very gently he withdrew a small way and pushed back into her. He repeated this until it was moving more easily for them both. The pain was less now, there was more of a numbness, but she felt a fullness inside her that replaced it.

He shifted his weight, and with a new angle his pelvis pressed against her, hitting just the right place each time he ground into her. It made her push back against his thrusts, meeting him in return.

"Feel how hard you make me."

His greater strength and her inability to resist him - had she even wanted to - made her more able to lose control. He was in command, he was doing this to her body, she was in his hands. She felt him inside her, each thrust going almost too deep but she wanted him as deep as possible.

He's my teacher, she thought. He was a grown adult and her superior on every level - age, experience, authority - yet something about this levelled them. The outside world faded away. Nothing else was.

The way he was grinding against her at the end of each thrust meant that just where it might have become uncomfortable, she instead got the pressure and stimulation she needed in front. It was less direct than when he touched her with his fingers but combined with the sensation of him inside her, filling her, it was enough.

Laura knew where her body was going, everyone had read Just Seventeen and other magazines and tried out their vague instructions at private moments. But this was nothing like touching herself. It was a thousand times more sensitive and she felt it throughout her stomach, not just between her legs.

It rose like a wave, she was pushing up towards him, and then the feeling started to peak and was running in spasms throughout her body. She clutched him, she was trembling, crying out. He seemed to know what she needed, and ground into her harder but more slowly.

Everything overtook her and she made noises she had not know she could make, soft, almost like crying.

Suddenly he pulled out of her and moved back over her, and she felt a warm, thick wetness fall over her stomach.

Laura lay there, her head and body dizzy, and he kissed her mouth and then lay down beside her.

"I wasn't expecting that we would go so fast, so soon. I get carried away around you, though that's no excuse. Did I hurt you?" he asked.

She didn't want to admit it because he might feel bad. "Only at the very start and then it was fine."

"I'm sorry." He stroked her cheek.

"Don't be, it was amazing. I haven't ever… I mean it was the first time, but I am so glad it was you. I didn't want you to stop."

She was babbling but she felt nervous. She wasn't sure what one was supposed to do next. Get up? Bathe? Sleep? She should have sought more detailed information from Susie. She was also worried that it was all over now and that he wouldn't want this again.

He rolled onto his side and faced her again. The sweat on her skin was cooling and she was just starting to feel colder. He noticed her stomach and grabbed a nearby towel.

"I'm sorry about that too, for losing control. Or nearly." When he had dried her he kissed her again and she enjoyed the warmth of his body.

Then he looked at her, and his eyes were grey and intense.

"I love you."

His words hung in the air. She couldn't breathe, her whole being sang with joy.

"Do you really?" She hadn't thought it possible for him to feel that way about her.

"Christ, of course I do. Do you think I could have done that to you if I didn't?"

"I love you too."

He put his arms around her and held her until she fell asleep.

14. Growing closer

Late autumn sunlight filtered through the gap in the curtain, waking her. She was alone in his bed, sticky, rumpled, sore.

For a moment she thought he had abandoned her and panicked.

Then he came into the room with a cup of tea.

"How are you?"

She was embarrassed for him to see her so dishevelled and tucked herself further below the sheet.

"About last night..." he began.

Oh God. He was going to tell her that it was all a mistake, that he regretted it. Maybe she had been terrible in bed.

"I didn't mean for everything to happen so quickly. I truly meant to take my time. The problem is that I lose control around you but it shouldn't be like that, I should have been far more gentle, your first time."

He came and sat down by her on the bed, putting the cup down on a table.

"I don't want to hurt you, but I'm worried about the reaction I have towards you. I wanted to be your first, to make you properly mine, and something overtook me."

She loved his possessiveness. "I didn't ask you to stop."

"My fear is that I wouldn't have done, even if you had."

This gave Laura a shivery feeling inside, and she felt a throb between her legs.

"I don't mind though. I like it when you take control." She said this last almost in a whisper. He saw the desire in her eyes.

"Does it bother you that I'm not older?" she asked.

"I wish it bothered me more." He pulled the sheet back from her, revealing her body. He ran both his hands over her breasts, and her nipples peaked at his touch. "God, how I want you."

He rolled her onto her stomach, and stroked his hands down the contours of her back and waist. It was soothing and electrifying. She felt him kiss her down her spine. All the points of her body that she wanted him to touch - her nipples, between her legs - were facing downwards and inaccessible. She squirmed against the sheet.

He put his hands on her thighs, and parted them. "I know you're probably sore, but I have to have you. I will be gentle," he said.

She was sore and it stung as he started to push into her from behind, but she wanted it too. He entered her as slowly as he could, fraction by fraction, giving her time to adjust. "Christ you're so tight, does it hurt?"

"A little. But don't stop."

She felt him stretching her, filling her. The slowness made her feel it even more than the previous evening.

She knew - she could hear it in his voice - that a dark part of him wanted to hurt her, to dominate her. To make her his. And the knowledge of it made her able to abandon herself to him.

He covered her back with his body, and she was completely filled by him. He rocked back and forth into her in small movements, still slowly. She felt the hugeness of him inside her, the weight above.

"I don't want you to ever fuck anyone else but me."

The harshness of his language only heightened her sensations.

Then he put his hands around her waist and drove into her fast and hard, over and over and over, until they were both spent.

* * *

The rest of Saturday passed in a kind of haze. Laura felt an intense joy just to be around him. She didn't dare go outside in case she was seen by a teacher, as many staff stayed on the school grounds over exeat weekends.

They were trapped together. The cottage was a bunker amid the storm clouds gathering. He asked her if she wanted to watch television but she didn't want to let the outside world in, to break the spell.

He had some marking to do, so she looked through his bookshelf to find something to read. Its contents were mainly in German. Most of his books were in storage, he told her. "There are some novels by the bed."

They weren't by authors that Laura had ever read, though she had heard of some of them. One was by P G Wodehouse with a cover illustration of cricketers, so she chose that one.

He noticed the cover when she came back down with it. "You like cricket? Or Wodehouse?"

"I've never read him. But I've played cricket with my cousins."

She had barely had time to read the first pages when he threw down his marking and came over to her.

"Companionable silence isn't working for me." He put his hand under her top and felt her breast. "I want you again."

She loved him touching her, loved him wanting her, loved his intensity even as it frightened her.

"Take your clothes off," he said.

"Here?"

"Now."

It was an order, not a request. Not that she would have refused him.

She stood there naked; he was fully clothed.

For a while he gazed at her. It may have only been moments, it felt like several minutes. Then he came up to her. He put her hands on either side of her head and tilted it to look at his.

She couldn't read his expression. For a moment she thought he was going to devour her. Crush her in a kiss, bruise her skin in his grip.

Instead his lips were on hers softly and he kissed her slowly and tenderly. Then down her neck and on her shoulder. He moved around her body as though it were a statue, kissing her in places that made her feel dizzy to her feet.

She felt revered.

Then he was before her again, kissing her neck, her breasts, her stomach as he knelt down in front of her.

He moved her legs slightly more apart, and as she stood there he kissed her between them, and she felt his tongue move into the slit between them. It was so much softer than his fingers and lacked their pressure but when he swirled it around her clitoris she gasped slightly and nearly lost her balance.

He broke off and looked up at her. "Stand still. You're going to come for me right here."

The command nearly brought her to the edge, and then he was tasting her again. Deliberately not using his fingers, just licking her and sucking her.

She gripped his shoulders to stay upright. Being in this position and feeling all the blood swelling in her groin made her light headed. She rocked slightly and he went harder on her clit and it was enough.

She reached her peak, moaning, her leg muscles tensing as he continued what he was doing, not even stopping as the spasms subsided and it was too sensitive in an instant.

Then her knees buckled slightly and a grey fuzziness spread before her eyes like a broken television picture, and she closed them and he had to catch her as she nearly fainted.

Still dizzy, he moved her to the sofa, bent her over the edge and thrust into her.

* * *

"Will it be weird in class? Will people guess?"

They were lying on the sofa together naked with only the light and heat of the gas fire.

"It will be normal. I'll be as distracted by you as ever - more than ever - but you won't know a thing and nor will anyone else," he said.

"I will." She could tell when he wanted her from his eyes, she didn't need the more obvious physical signs to know how he felt.

He stroked her breast, playing with her nipple. He never seemed to tire of her body.

They hadn't really talked about what happened next. "After this weekend, will you want to... again?" she asked him.

"Laura, you're mine now. I will always want you."

There was a note in the way he said "mine" that made her shiver.

She let him know how she felt by kissing him. She was learning to initiate.

"We'll have to be very careful," he said. "But we will make it work."

15. Confession

Not wanting to push her luck, Laura slipped back to Michaelmas House earlier than she needed to on Sunday night, among the first girls arriving back.

She was worried everyone would notice, that what she had done was written all over her face. She even felt she was walking differently. Her head and her body were in a different place now.

Part of her wanted space and time to process everything while the rest was longing for the fellowship of her dorm mates. She knew she wouldn't be able to hide anything from Susie.

She sat on her bed, looking out of the window across the darkening playing fields. She could see the light on the groundsman's cottages. And for a while she was perfectly at peace.

Charlotte was the first to burst in. "What a weekend! Almost a relief to be back in school." She threw her bag on the floor and collapsed on the other window bed.

"Not a good one?"

"Just a round-the-clock grilling over everything I didn't get an A-plus in," Charlotte said. "I should have had more nerve and gone with Susie to St Duncan's."

Margery came in next and in her usual fashion immediately began hanging up her clothes and tidying away her other effects.

"Relax Margie, there's no inspection today," Charlotte said.

"I just like things tidy." Margery didn't ask them about their weekend, she was still feeling aggrieved at being dropped by Laura.

Susie arrived wreathed in sly smiles. She had had the best time ever, she told them, and won a load of money playing poker. "Fifty quid the first night, and fifty quid last night when they tried to win it back from me. They can afford it," she said, seeing Margery's alarmed face. "And it's a good lesson for them. Better fifty quid to me than fifty grand in Monte Carlo."

Laura marvelled at Susie. She had no idea herself how to even play poker. How did Susie get to be so sophisticated? She supposed it was something to do with spending summers in Italy with her wealthy relatives. They owned vineyards.

"So what about all you girls?" Susie said. "Laura?" Susie had a particularly knowing grin on her face.

Crunch time had come. Laura knew she could trust them, but what she had to reveal was so huge. Would it wreck their friendship? What if they disapproved?

"Well..." she began, not sure how even to start.

"Brace yourselves," Susie said. "This is a big one."

Margery looked at them both in bewilderment. "What's going on?"

Laura couldn't take a deep breath because her chest felt so tense she could hardly get any air in. Staring at the floor, she said quickly and quietly:

"I spent the weekend with Mr Rydell."

There was a pause. Margery frowned and Charlotte burst out laughing. "Yeah, right."

"No, I really did. At his place."

Charlotte looked at Susie who was smiling like the Sphinx and then back at Laura. She saw how pale Laura looked, and the nervousness in her eyes.

"Christ, Christ, Christ on a bike. Bloody Hell. You're not joking? What and when and how and why, and why didn't you tell us?"

When had it started? Laura wasn't even sure where to begin.

She did her best. How she'd liked him from the start and felt a connection with him. How he'd stopped and talked with her several times. How they'd been alone in his classroom. How it had suddenly… just happened. And how he had asked her to stay with him that weekend. She didn't even get to the details of what happened.

"He's your teacher, Laura. He's so old. It's just wrong." Margery was distressed and confused.

Charlotte was shocked but fascinated. "He is so gorgeous. I just can't believe he would go for someone not even in the sixth form. This is true right? I mean this isn't some joke between you and Susie?"

Susie was getting impatient. "So did it go well this weekend? Did you guys do it? Was he any good?"

Laura went red.

"Welcome to the club then," Susie said. "You can give us a detailed account when you're ready." What she meant was when Margery wasn't there, as Margery would only be horrified rather than intrigued by the details.

She left the room, and Charlotte fired dozens more questions at Laura, mainly pertaining to the early days of the affair. "I just can't figure out how it could all have been going on under my nose."

Laura did her best to answer her questions. She was relieved that Charlotte wasn't aggrieved at being kept in the dark, and didn't seem to be against it all, unlike Margery.

"Nothing was actually happening, so there was nothing to see."

"But there must have been all these hidden undercurrents. Why didn't anyone else pick up on it?"

Laura cast a glance at Margery, who was folding away clothes. "I noticed him always staring at her," Margery said. "But I never thought anything like this would happen."

She was actually upset. She genuinely disapproved. Laura felt a pang.

"Neither did I, not in a million years. It just got to the point that nothing else mattered." She wanted Margery to understand. But Margery had never been in love, let alone reciprocally.

"He kissed you in his classroom. What if someone had seen you?"

This was what Laura had been trying to explain. How when it happened that wasn't even a consideration, not in the moment. Afterwards of course it became a terrifying concern.

Charlotte wanted to ask Laura for more of the juicy details of the past weekend, but Margery was putting a dampener on things. She and Susie would have to wait until they could get Laura alone.

* * *

"You're not going to sleep for hours, are you?" Susie said to Laura when they were in the bathroom. There was a shared area with a row of basins separate from the bath and shower rooms. "Me neither, but then I never do. Let's go out on the fire escape again."

Outside it was freezing cold, but they had wrapped up with dressing gowns and sat huddled on the hard ironwork of the stairs.

"So tell me all about it," Susie said. "I assume you actually did it. Was he any good?"

"I don't really have anything to compare it to."

"Did you enjoy it? Did he get you off?"

Laura covered her face in her hands, feeling embarrassed.

"I'll take that as a yes," Susie said. "At least with a older guy they should have some idea of what to do. Probably the best way to lose it really, instead of some schoolboy fumbling around."

"Darius wasn't like that was he?" Laura asked.

"I wouldn't know, we haven't gone there yet. I expect he's pretty au fait with what to do since he's dated older girls."

Laura was surprised how nonchalant Susie was about Darius's history. She herself felt uncomfortable thinking about how inexperienced she herself was compared to Mr Rydell.

"Does he want to see you again?" Susie asked.

"Yes, but I don't know when. We haven't arranged anything."

"Let me know when you do, I'm happy to cover for you if you like."

Laura looked through the darkness to the edge of the building, where it blocked the view of the groundsman's cottages. Strange to think he was only a few hundred yards from her. Was he asleep? Or awake, reading or working late?"

"He told me he loved me," she said.

"Wow." Susie was impressed. "It makes sense though given the risk he's taking. You don't just do that on a whim. Unless you're Mr Peters."

Laura laughed. "He's so creepy. I can't believe so many Sixth Form girls have fallen for him in the past."

Susie shuddered. "More fool them. Any St Duncan's boy would be better than that."

"Don't you worry at all about getting found out?" Laura asked Susie. "If you got caught with Darius I mean, and expelled."

"No, not really."

"Wouldn't your parents be mad?"

"No madder than before. They'd send me somewhere else again, and I'd see how I liked it," Susie said.

"My parents would be devastated." With the euphoria wearing off, Laura was starting to worry.

"You can stop you know, if it's more stress than it's worth."

Could she? Laura felt she was a different person now. She couldn't undo what was done. The funny thing was that she also felt more like her old self than she had done in weeks. Since she first saw him. He had changed her into something new, and yet part of her had been changed back.

* * *

Margery lay in her bed, desperately unhappy. She had been woken by the sounds of Laura and Susie creeping out. She had no idea where they were going. Charlotte was fast asleep.

She felt lonelier than ever. All the others seemed to think what Laura was doing was fascinating and wonderful, but it worried her sick. It didn't help that her own father was a teacher, and a languages teacher as well. Somehow she felt it to be a personal wrong.

Then there was this awful dance in a couple of weeks' time. Her dread at the thought of it was growing. If there was any way she could have escaped it she would have done so. If only it was on the Friday night she could have got her father to pick her up early for half-term.

But the Lower School dance was on the Thursday night, so she had no choice but to endure it. And endure the next day of gossiping and post mortems which in many ways would be even worse.

Could she pretend to be ill? She had foresight enough to know that Grace Grant would smell a rat at the timing, and practically force her to go.

She hadn't managed to buy anything more suitable to wear at the weekend. And she couldn't explain it to her father because he would just say that she had lots of clothes. The thought of the rah-rah skirt, hanging in the wardrobe, hung even more heavily on her heart. She would be a laughing stock.

* * *

Laura had deliberately not showered that evening so the memory of Mr Rydell would still be all over her skin for one more night. Still chilled from the cold night air she hugged herself under the blankets, wishing she was with him. They hadn't made any concrete plans of when and where to meet next.

Her diary had been sadly neglected but it had fulfilled its purpose. Its pages were no good to her anymore now her fantasies had risen off them.

It was also far too dangerous to write anything down.

She lay there, her body yearning for him. He had flicked a switch on that she couldn't turn off. She burned for him, his company as well as his touch. It had only been a few hours since she had left him but it already felt like days.

16. Stolen moments

When Laura walked into the German classroom Mr Rydell caught her eye and smiled. It was very brief but it was enough. They were good. They were a "they".

The whole lesson felt electric to her. She had this huge secret that almost no one else knew anything about. The man at the blackboard was no longer merely her German teacher. He had chosen her. She knew what he looked like naked, how it felt to be kissed by him, how his body felt against hers.

Looking at him, tall and authoritative, explaining some elements of German grammar, she wanted to be with him so badly it hurt.

It was impossible to put these thoughts out of her mind, but Laura was still just about able to concentrate on the lesson. It would have helped if Charlotte hadn't kept nudging her every other minute.

At the end of the lesson he asked her to stay behind.

"I know I have to avoid singling you out, but I couldn't let you go today without making sure you were okay," he said.

She told him she was fine.

"The weekend was amazing. You were amazing. I spent most of the lesson wishing I could dismiss the class and take you away for a repeat performance."

She saw the heat in his eyes. He didn't risk touching her as there would be people walking past the classroom at this time.

"Half term is just another couple of weeks away. Can you come back a couple of days early - say you're staying with a friend - and stay with me? If I can even hold out that long."

Laura smiled at him. She loved that he wanted her so much. "I'll manage it."

"Great. I can pick you up from wherever you need. And you have my number."

She had memorised it by heart.

"You'd better run to your next class. If I can figure out something for this week, I will."

Her heart singing, she hurried off.

* * *

Charlotte was waiting for her around the corner. "Everything okay?"

"All good."

"That's a relief. I wasn't sure if he was going to change his mind on you again. I was watching for smouldering glances but he seemed very well controlled."

"He wants me to stay with him at the end of half-term," Laura told her. "I can't use Margery again though."

"I think she'd still agree, but it is awkward. I wish I could help. What about Susie?"

"I'll ask her. She said earlier it should be ok."

They walked onto the next class which was Maths. Susie had bagsed them desks on the back row. She was eager to find out how German had gone with Laura seeing Mr Rydell again.

"You must really regret picking Geography instead," Charlotte said.

"Yes and no. Geography has its charms."

Charlotte could think of few things less charming than Mrs Ayers.

"She is a problem," Susie agreed.

The maths lesson started, and they were forced to stop talking.

* * *

Margery was sitting in the Michaelmas Lower School common room with her sewing basket and the dreaded rah-rah skirt, trying to find some way to make it look more presentable for the dance. She was close to despair.

Pride held her back from asking the others for help. A wall had gone up since her disapproval of Laura's relationship with Mr Rydell. It was a wall entirely built by Margery because the others didn't mind that Margery minded. Laura actually felt bad that Margery was upset about it. But Margery struggled with it, and the distance grew.

It was here that Teresa Hubert chanced upon her. "Mending something?" She noticed that Margery had some sequins and guessed what was up. "You're not going to wear that to the dance, are you? You really can't wear that. Didn't you find a dress on exeat?"

Margery heart slumped further with misery.

Teresa saw her opportunity. "I'm sure we can find you a dress. Andrea has two. She's still deciding which to wear. I'm sure you'll fit the other."

Teresa had two henchwomen, one small, one large and lumpen. This latter was Andrea. Margery was mortified to be put in a size bracket with her. Teresa herself was thin in a spindly way.

But the offer of a dress was a lifeline in a storm. "She wouldn't mind?" Margery asked. She had no idea what the dress would be like, but anything was better than a knee-length rah-rah skirt. Even a fourth former wouldn't want to wear that.

"She'd only be too happy." What Teresa meant was that she would only be too happy for Andrea to lend the dress, so Teresa would finally have some leverage over Margery. Andrea wouldn't be given any choice over whether she lent it or not.

* * *

There were a few stolen moments. The art room, which was usually left open but was frequently unoccupied, was nearby the Modern Languages block. They met there a couple of times during break.

It was too risky to go the whole way in broad daylight with the chance that Mr Lanaway might flit in on a whim. But the need for restraint only increased their need for one another.

Even making out fully clothed Mr Rydell could bring Laura to orgasm, and often quickly. His lips on hers, his hand between her thighs, taking control of her body. She was totally at his mercy.

He knew that when he spoke to her and told her to do things that it pushed her to the edge. And he liked commanding her.

He would tell her that she had to wait, and remove the pressure of his fingers, and she would push back desperately against him to regain it. "I can't wait, don't make me wait," she begged him.

And he would keep embracing her, caressing her through her uniform, but avoiding the point of pleasure that she so urgently craved.

"What do you want from me, Laura? Tell me what you want?"

She found it hard at first to tell him, but desire overtook her inhibitions.

"I want you to touch me."

"Where?"

"There." She pushed his hand where she wanted it, pressing towards him as he teased her with his lips on her neck, on the skin that was bare to him above the collar of her blouse.

"Tell me exactly where. And exactly what you want."

"Please, touch my clit." She found it unbearable to say at first, but he wouldn't give her what she wanted unless she asked for it.

"Like this?"

"Yes, and don't stop. Please don't stop." And she would collapse in his arms, dizzy yet still not satiated because she ached to have him fully inside her.

And then they would have to part, taking it in turns to leave first as they couldn't be seen leaving together, and each time she felt it like a physical pain.

* * *

Mr Peters was still hankering after Susie Clarke. He had reshuffled his casting for The Merchant of Venice, and Susie was now reading Portia while he had recast himself as Antonio.

He was also planning for the class to read some non-curriculum scenes of his own choosing as a little treat for the end of term. Or perhaps he could squeeze them in just before half term? After all it would be helpful for the girls to be better acquainted with other works of Shakespeare, such as Romeo and Juliet, so they had a better appreciation of the play when they watched the Sixth Form production later on. Susanna would read Juliet so perfectly.

The Head of English had no idea what an absurd figure he was to the class. In private he imagined her on his couch, as he seduced her with the sonnets of the Bard. How to get her there was the issue. He lacked no confidence in his charms if he could only lure her to his flat. If only there was some kind of extra tuition that could be offered, but frustratingly Susie excelled easily at English.

Perhaps he might offer some one-on-one coaching for Miss Wingrove's poetry recital. The woman could hardly obstruct this. After all, he was the Head of Department. He wondered what Susie had chosen to read. Perhaps he might introduce her to some of the metaphysical poets.

He imagined declaiming Marvell's To His Coy Mistress to the girl. He would enjoy her inevitable blushes at "long preserv'd virginity" and "tear our pleasures".

* * *

Susie had moved into the second phase of her campaign against Mrs Ayers. Things started disappearing from the Geography teacher's classroom, or showing up in unusual places. Her chalk didn't work properly, or snapped. The board eraser had grease all over it. There were always drawing pins turning up, sometimes she stepped on them, other times she reached for something and had one pricking her. One day her chair leg collapsed as she sat down in front of the class. When she demanded that Jenkins inspect it, he found nothing except a loose screw that he suggested may have happened by itself.

Foul smells started to emanate, eventually causing the classroom to be evacuated. The odour was finally traced to the curtains, but there was no obvious trace of anything inside them. Mrs Grayson herself checked the hems. If anything had been put there, it had long since been removed.

They were petty, puerile tricks, but it was the volume and constancy of them that had a devastating impact. Mrs Ayers' fury and paranoia grew simultaneously. She was certain Susie was behind them, but could never catch her.

The two them remained deadlocked in loathing: Mrs Ayers lashing out with demerits and detentions and sending Susie out of the class for imaginary offences such as dabbing her nose with a tissue, or closing her pencil box "deliberately loudly", and Susie continuing her irreproachable schoolwork and secret campaign of torment.

* * *

Charlotte was finally trying out for the senior squad. It was a while since a Lower School girl had done so but Miss Partridge handled it in a deliberately low key manner. She simply called her to practice with the squad one afternoon. "I'd like you to come to play with the seniors on Wednesday."

Charlotte knew this was it. She was searing with determination. Nothing else mattered. Yet she had to make sure her schoolwork was perfect so there couldn't be any excuse, any obstacle, for not letting her play.

"You're getting more studious than Margery these days," Laura said. "First Latin, then all the running, now this."

"I don't have a choice. It's all or nothing."

She had to be careful she didn't burn herself out.

* * *

If truth be told Susie was a little bored and tired. The warfare with Mrs Ayers was draining, along with losing her freedom every Saturday afternoon. But it needed to be sustained for a while longer.

Mr Peters' incessant lechery was also a drag, nothing she couldn't deal with, but it would have to come to a head at some point. Somehow she would need to turn that to her advantage.

Exeat had been amusing with the boys at St Duncan's and now there was this dance that everyone was so excited about, but it wasn't Susie's idea of fun. Unfortunately her options for entertainment were limited.

Susie didn't want to be at school. She wanted to go and work for her uncle in the family business, but her father wouldn't hear of it until she turned eighteen. That was years away. She wouldn't even be sixteen until the second half of term.

So she figured if she couldn't do anything for herself, she may as well help the others. Laura's fling with the German teacher amused her. Surprised her even. Not so much that Laura had been bowled over - who wouldn't be in her shoes? - but that Mr Rydell had yielded. He really didn't seem the type. He was no Mr Peters, certainly.

What were his motives? she wondered. Susie couldn't conceive of people not having motives even if they were unaware of them themselves.

If they got caught, and to her mind it was inevitable that unless this thing burned out quickly they would, his career would be over and Laura would be expelled. He was a grown man, he'd survive, but she wasn't sure if Laura would. Having mutually agreed to leave several schools herself - they'd never quite termed it expulsion - she knew what Laura was in for. And Laura wasn't like her. It would break her.

17. Slow dance

"I need you to create a diversion so I can get inside," Susie said.

"What are you talking about? You passed the dress inspection." It was the night of the Lower School dance and they were all glammed up and ready to party.

But Susie had seen Mrs Ayers by the door. Even had she dressed in a burqa the Axe would have found fault enough to bar her.

"Trust me. She will never let me in. Scream, faint, anything. Just get the Axe away from the door."

Laura was puzzled. She knew Susie had some feud with the Axe, but she could hardly imagine things were this bad. She did what she could. "Mrs Ayers, I don't want to be a tattletale, but I think I smelt someone smoking in the bushes."

Mrs Ayers stormed off, rage mixing with grim pleasure at the prospect of apprehending the culprit. The chance to excoriate some girl took priority over holding her own secondary dress inspection at the door. She had suspected Grace Grant would let her girls get away with murder.

Susie saw her chance and slipped in.

* * *

Grace Grant had in fact wrestled with herself over Susie's attire. It wasn't that there was anything about it that broke the rules; in fact it was arguably more modest than many of the other girls' dresses. It was just... so sophisticated. So suggestive. The housemistress wasn't closely across the latest fashion on the catwalks of Milan but she suspected that Susie's frock wasn't long off them.

It was black, clearly designer, and even more clearly designed for a woman at least ten years older than Susie. Unfortunately Susie filled it admirably well, with the result that even with minimal make up she looked about twenty-five.

"That dress will rewrite the rules," Grace Grant thought, predicting even more draconian guidelines for future non-uniform events.

She felt proud of most of the girls and happy for them. Even the plain Janes were glowing tonight. Margery was wearing Andrea's slightly-too-roomy velvet cast-off, but was so relieved not to be in her dreaded rah-rah that she was lit up. In a quiet way she was a pretty girl, particularly with the cross-country running having burned off some of her puppy fat.

Charlotte looked spectacular in emerald taffeta. She was the tallest girl in the year and recently seemed to have embraced her height.

And Laura. Grace Grant didn't know what to make of Laura. She was in midnight blue and black and looked exceptionally pretty. Beautiful, even. But there was something more. The only way that the housemistress could describe it was that Laura reminded her of Susie.

* * *

"Will you dance with us Sir?"

Mr Poynter's round face was already perspiring as he tried to disco dance amid a group of girls. Despite the presence of the St Duncan's boys the male teachers were usually in strong demand. Even Mr Lanaway had been dragged onto the floor.

Susie made a beeline for Mr Rydell. "Won't you dance with us? All the other teachers are."

"You're not even in my class, are you?" But he knew she was Laura's friend and was doing this for her.

Being face-to-face with one another, albeit with the chaperonage of the rest of the group, was electric. He had never seen Laura dressed up and Susie had done a spectacular job helping her get ready.

Laura wanted to dance just for him, wanted everyone else to dissolve. Looking into his eyes she knew he felt the same. Trying to sneak out would be insanity, they would just have to be patient.

He couldn't spend more than a couple of songs with them, he was technically on duty.

They danced among themselves and with some of the St Duncan's boys. Charlotte and Susie had something of a prestige among them since it was known that they were dating sixth form prefects. The younger boys still danced with them but kept their distance.

"Why's Margery spending so much time with Teresa Hubert?" Charlotte asked.

"She borrowed Andrea's dress," Susie said. Laura felt guilty as she knew it was partly her fault that Margery had nearly been without one.

Margery felt neutral at the dance which was a step up from the misery she had expected. She didn't dance with any of the boys but she was very content to feel that she looked normal.

Susie was aware of Mrs Ayer's gimlet eye on her, but she ignored it. She was behaving as perfectly as she could. She itched to liven up the night by dancing on a table or spiking the punch but she restrained herself.

At the end of the night there was a single slow number, the only song where people danced as couples. This was still extremely chaste: any boy and girl dancing too close together received swift intervention. It was unofficially known as the "six inch rule".

Now time for my supreme sacrifice, Susie thought. Dragging Laura and Charlotte with her she marched up to where some of the teachers were standing by the side of the room.

"You'll dance with me won't you Mr Poynter?" Susie grabbed the history teacher, and whirled him round onto the dancefloor. Charlotte followed her cue, and reluctantly danced with the equally reluctant Mr Lanaway.

That left Laura with a green light to dance one-on-one with Mr Rydell. Best of all, they could talk.

"You look beautiful, it's been torture all night not being able to speak to you," he said. "Though as beautiful as that dress is, I would like to rip it right off you."

Laura hoped no one could lip-read. She had to concentrate on trying to keep dancing as she wanted to just stand there and gaze at him.

"Then I would like to run my hands all over your body, until you were begging me to make love to you right on the middle of this dancefloor." He was smiling lightly as he spoke, so anyone watching them would have assumed he was making general conversation.

"And if you had read Goethe, you would know that quote," he continued.

Laura was momentarily confused then realised that Mr Poynter had just passed within earshot.

They were playing with fire.

"Go on then, do it now," she challenged him when the History teacher had moved by. "In front of everyone."

She moved her hands to her own body as she spoke, swaying her hips and smiling at him.

His eyes narrowed and she realised how nearly she could bring him to the edge of losing control. They both knew that he would deal with her hard, later.

* * *

"I'm not sure if that was entirely wise, dancing one-on-one with the girls," Miss Wingrove remarked to him later.

"I couldn't see the harm. And Charles was getting into the swing," he said, referring to Mr Poynter.

"You're not Charles Poynter. Even he ought to know better. I know this lot are only Lower School, but in an all-girls school, at this age, they're touch paper. Just be careful."

At least he was no Mr Peters, Miss Wingrove thought. Thank God he hadn't been here tonight, with Susie Clarke wearing that incredibly inappropriate dress.

Mr Peters had already approached the other English teacher with his offer to coach the participants in her poetry recital. Miss Wingrove was well aware that there was only one pupil he was interested in coaching, and it certainly wasn't to improve her poetic performance.

* * *

The excitement lasted well into the night with hardly anyone observing silence after lights out. Many had swapped addresses with St Duncan's boys and the excitement of half term lay ahead. Just one more day.

"I can't believe you three choosing teachers for the slow dance," someone said to Charlotte. "What a complete waste."

"Not if I get an A in history," Susie said.

Laura was incredibly grateful to her but Susie waved off her thanks. "It's not as though we were interested in any of those boys anyway. And at least you got some time with your man."

Her man. The phrase thrilled Laura, though she didn't know if she was entitled to it. Sneaking around all the time prevented her from feeling official.

"He looked like he wanted to ravish you right there. Don't worry, no one else would have noticed," she said as Laura looked alarmed.

They had bigger plans for the next night. Julian and Darius would be at the Sixth Form dance and planned to sneak out and meet them. Along with Jonathan, the boy Laura had kissed. She was going to have to let him down gently somehow, find some excuse. She could hardly tell him the truth.

18. Mistaken

It was the Sixth Form girls' turn for fun, but Susie and Charlotte bided their time. The fact that they had taken two of the biggest prizes would not go down well with the older girls so they'd had to keep things discreet.

"Won't we look awful if they meet us in school uniform and all the Sixth Formers are done up to the nines?" Charlotte said.

"They won't care. It will be dark anyway."

Margery wasn't actively involved in their plans, but was secretly wondering and hoping if the boy she had liked might be there.

Laura had rehearsed various break up phrases in her head. She had sought Susie's input to little avail as she had dismissed all of Laura's ideas.

"You can't say 'it's not you, it's me' as everyone knows that's a lie. And you can't tell him that your studies are too demanding because that's obviously a lie to. And 'it's just not working' won't do because let's face it, there's nothing really happening to work or not, is there? A letter or so every month."

Susie's suggestion was to take a leaf from the Queen Mother's book and simply "never apologise, never explain."

But Laura couldn't be quite that harsh.

* * *

Not having late prep on the eve of the holiday made it easier for them to sneak out of Michaelmas House to the main school.

They had arranged to meet the St Duncan's boys at eight o'clock by the side of the hall. It was a cold night and Laura felt miserable with nerves.

Jonathan looked really happy to see her which made her feel even worse. She walked with him around the corner, girding herself for the difficult conversation. Unaware, he put his arms around her and went to kiss her. "Don't," she said.

Before she could start explaining she looked up. Mr Rydell stood there, just a short distance away.

His face was like ice.

He came over to them. "Neither of you should be here. Get back to the hall immediately," he told Jonathan who shot her a worried, apologetic look and left.

"And you, this way."

He dragged her to the nearby Art room which was unlocked.

Inside it was dark, lit only by lights shining through the window from outside. He didn't turn a light on. Instead he gripped her shoulders and kissed her savagely. His mouth bruised hers, his teeth grazed her lips.

She was thrilled to be with him, relieved that he wasn't rejecting her, but terrified of his anger. "It wasn't what you think," she began when he broke off.

"I don't care what it is, Laura, I need to make you understand why you are not going to mess around with some schoolboy."

"But..."

He silenced her again with his mouth on hers, tearing off his jacket. He pushed her against one of the tables and tugged her underwear down from under her skirt.

The smell of paint, the smell of clay. The same clay she had used to mould a figurine shaped like him.

She couldn't stop him even if she had wanted to. His hands were already possessing her.

"It doesn't take much to get you wet, does it? Was that for him or me?"

She couldn't believe the effect he had on her. Even being brutal he turned her core to liquid.

He had thrust two fingers inside her, feeling how wet she was, already lubricated enough for him. Removing them, he pushed her down on the table, and replaced them with his full length.

She cried out at the suddenness and the size of him. He didn't allow her a moment to get used to it.

He had never been this forceful before. He drove into her, as hard as he could, again and again, trying to own her, trying to punish her. He gripped her wrists and held her arms above her head so she couldn't move, couldn't fight him.

He twisted as he thrust into her, screwing into her as deep as possible. He wanted to hurt her as much as he wanted to bring her over the edge, so she knew that he had command of her, dominion over her body.

And she was lost. Nothing but raw feeling. Her heart ached for him as much as her body throbbed.

"You are mine. Mine, mine," he repeated as he pushed into her.

"Yes!" she cried out to him as her body took over.

"Come for me, Laura, come for me now."

She had never orgasmed so hard. She was practically sobbing, clinging to him.

Just as it started to happen he climaxed too, enhancing her own sensations. It was the first time they had come together, he usually got her there first.

Then staying inside her he slumped on top of her, and she felt his weight crushing her body. She could only just breathe.

"God, forgive me, forgive me, I am so sorry. I never wanted to hurt you," he said.

She wasn't sure how long they lay there for, in the near darkness, the hard surface of the art table beneath her and his body above.

Eventually he got up from her and helped her up. He held her to him and stroked her hair. Tenderly.

"It wasn't what you thought," she said.

"It's okay, you don't have to explain."

But she told him anyway. How Jonathan had never been any more than a penpal, that she had been about to let him down, that she no interest in him or any other boys.

"And I took my anger out on you like that. What have I come to, a grown man getting jealous of some schoolboy?" He was truly contrite, hating himself.

She tried to make it better. "I felt bad that you misunderstood and I couldn't explain, but you didn't hurt me," she said.

"I forced myself on you in anger, I practically raped you."

"You knew - you could tell - I wanted you too. Otherwise you wouldn't have done."

"Wouldn't I?"

She looked at his face, the dark, deep shadows under its angles. His hair fell over his brow, he looked haunted with guilt.

She felt anxious. "Do you still...?"

"Love you? Christ yes. I am going out of my mind with what I feel for you. Look what it's doing to me."

She had meant to ask him if he still wanted to see her, or if he regretted it too much to continue, but his answer was more than she could have hoped for.

* * *

He took a risk and walked back with her towards Michaelmas House, until he needed to take the other path to the groundsman's cottages. He couldn't bear to let her go alone.

She loved the darkness for giving them cover. It was a starless, moonless night. It had rained earlier and the tarmac still glistened under the street lights.

"I hate leaving you, particularly after the way I treated you."

"I wish I could just come back with you. I could sneak out in the morning."

But it was too much risk.

"Just six more days and we get to spend the whole weekend together. Not that I'll find it easy waiting," he said.

They stood briefly before their paths diverged.

"This is me wanting to take you in my arms and kiss you and tell you how sorry I am and how much I love you, but not daring to in the remote chance someone can see this far in the dark and is watching us," he said.

"This is me doing the same."

"Sleep well, I will think of you all night."

* * *

Back in the dorm Susie convulsed with laughter when Laura gave them a brief account of what had happened.

"We wondered what had happened to you. Jonathan passed us on the way back in and looked absolutely terrified. From the way he described it we thought it must have been Mr Tyrrell who found you. Too funny that it was Mr Rydell!"

"So did you manage to explain everything to him? Was he mad?" Charlotte asked.

It was written all over Laura's face though she had intended not to reveal anything.

"Oh my God you fucked him in the art room!" Susie said. "How are we supposed to concentrate the next time we do ceramics?"

She had enjoyed her stolen half hour with Darius, and Charlotte had managed to go further with Julian than with any of her Welsh boys over the summer. She was quite starry-eyed about him.

Margery had been on the edges of the conversation, not saying anything. She felt terribly left out. But she also burned to know if the boy she liked had been there. She screwed up her courage.

"Was Robert there?"

"We didn't see him. Honestly it's not you, Margie, I don't think he really goes after anyone. He's shy, Darius said."

Susie was lying to save Margery's feelings. In actual fact Darius had said that he wasn't interested.

The last thing Laura remembered before she fell asleep was that he hadn't used any protection. Thank God her period was due.

19. Out of bounds

He met her at the station and she ran into his arms. It had been the longest week of her life. They had managed to phone each other once or twice, but it was hard because the phone at Laura's house was in the living room. It was difficult to get any privacy.

Carrying her bag, he walked her outside to his car.

"Your parents don't suspect anything?"

"No, they were just glad for me that a friend had asked me to stay." Susie was her alibi for the weekend.

Before he started the engine, he turned to her. "So I figured as it was the holiday, there was no point just going back to school. How would you like to go up to London for a couple of days?"

"Really?" She would absolutely love it.

"We can do whatever we want, no sneaking around. See whatever you want to see."

Laura's first thought was Madame Tussaud's and a whole host of other tourist sites that she had always wanted to visit. Her family lived so far from London that she had only been there a couple of times. She didn't want to sound like a child though. "The British Museum?"

"You'd really like to go there? I was thinking more along the lines of the Tower of London or the Zoo. But we can easily visit the Museum if you want. There's plenty of time."

"Actually I would really like to see Madame Tussaud's."

He laughed. "Then we'll do that."

"Where will we stay?"

"I'll get us a hotel. The Ritz if you like."

She wasn't sure if he was joking. She also remembered that she had hardly any money with her. Suddenly it all seemed huge, she felt out of her depth. She was familiar with the confines of school, comfortable with its restrictions. But this - a hotel - just the two of them in the city for an entire weekend, was she ready for it? She tried to think like Susie, who would doubtless have demanded the Royal Suite and champagne and made a ball of it.

She stared out of the window. They were already on the motorway.

He picked up on her anxiety. "What's worrying you?"

"Nothing, it's just I haven't really got much money with me."

"Laura, you don't have to pay for a thing. I earn a wage, you don't. Nor does that put you under any obligation to me. Of course if you want to feel obligated..." He was joking, but he put his hand on her thigh, and moved it up. "Pity you're not wearing a skirt, this would be a lot easier."

"You can't do this here, you'll crash."

He opened the front of her jeans and pushed his hand down below her underwear, making her squirm in her seat. His fingers found exactly what they sought, and he applied just the right pressure.

"I can't! Not in broad daylight," she said.

"You can and you will."

God. She closed her eyes and bit her lip. He moved his fingers over her, feeling her increased wetness at his touch.

"I'm not going to stop until you're there."

He loved making her come, making her lose control from his touch.

"This is only the start. I want you every way tonight, Laura, I want all of you."

She didn't know exactly what he meant but she knew she could trust him. Her breathing was getting faster, she was almost too sensitive beneath his fingers, but he didn't relent.

It was such direct stimulation that it didn't take him long to bring her over the edge. She felt her face flush with heat.

He glanced at her. "You are so beautiful when you're aroused."

* * *

It was the first time she had stayed in a proper hotel. She wanted to look around at everything, but he threw her on the bed.

"Finally."

Her heart was already racing for him, she needed more than what he had done to her in the car.

"After a week without you this will probably be over in seconds, but we have all night," he said.

Afterward she lay in his arms, completely and utterly happy. She still found it hard to believe she was with him. He was so good looking, so intelligent, so tall and strong. So adult, compared to boys of her own age. What did he see in her? She wasn't even one of the glamorous girls at school. There were a couple of sixth form girls who practically looked like models.

Yet he loved her and wanted her.

Laura turned onto her side and looked at his face, leaning on her elbow. He opened his eyes. "What is it?"

She lent over him and kissed his lips. She played with them, nibbling his bottom lip. Then while he lay there she worked her way down his body. Down his neck, past his collarbone. Over the hard, defined planes of his chest. His stomach with the trail of dark hair leading her lower.

She hadn't ever done what she planned to do, and had no real idea how to do it, but she wanted to make him feel as he made her feel. He was already hard again from her kisses over his body, and she wondered at the size of him. They didn't cover this in Biology.

She took him in her mouth, kneeling over him. His skin tasted salty but it wasn't bad. Her hair fell down in a curtain, brushing against his stomach. He pushed it back, wanting to watch her.

Not really knowing what to do except to try and stimulate him as much as she could with her tongue, she moved her head down and tried to take him deeper into her mouth. She swirled her tongue around him and he groaned.

By instinct she got into a kind of rhythm, moving her head, hand, and tongue on him, not really knowing where she was going but aware that she was having more and more effect on him. Then his hips bucked and he pulled her head off him and she watched as he came. She had never seen it before.

"Where did you learn how to do that?"

She was embarrassed to tell him it was the first time she had tried it.

"But how did you know what to do?" he asked.

"Magazines and stuff, you know." Susie had also told her a few things, but she didn't mention this to him. He knew that the others knew about them, after all she needed their help to be able to see him, but he didn't know exactly what details she shared.

* * *

The Italian restaurant was crowded due to it being the weekend. The lighting was dim, with candles on each table. They had deliberately chosen somewhere not far from the hotel.

It was a day of firsts: after the hotel, this was the first time Laura had been out with him in public. She had initially felt nervous but he was so easy to be with.

They shared a pizza and got onto the topic of Susie. "We have her to thank for your alibi. It makes me uneasy though, asking one of your school friends to lie," he said.

Laura explained that Susie didn't care what happened to her.

"She has her future all mapped out. Her uncle's going to give her a job in his business as soon as she's eighteen, and she says she'll get to travel the world."

"They're in wine aren't they?"

"Yes. Her parents want her to go to university but she says she can do that later on. Business studies or commerce."

Susie was so clear-sighted about what she wanted. None of the others had nearly such a definite idea of what they planned to do. Margery thought she would probably become a teacher and Charlotte still hoped for something in sport but Laura herself had no idea beyond going to university.

"Oxford or Cambridge?"

"God no, I don't think so. Only a few people go for that every year."

"You could easily do so, you're already in all top sets," he said. "What would you do, English?"

"Probably. I wondered about History for a while. If I take them both for A-levels I can decide later on."

The waiter came to top up their wine. Laura didn't usually drink much alcohol. Unlike many of her friends she had never even been drunk. She was already feeling tired and light headed but took a gamble on one more glass.

"If you do want to do Oxbridge I'll coach you," he said.

"But you did languages."

"It's no different, it's all literature. And I'd feel less guilt about taking advantage of you if I was benefitting your education rather than wrecking it."

$$* * *$$

Laura's head was swimming from the wine and she felt woozy from tiredness. She just wanted to fall asleep in bed with him but she knew he wanted her badly. The desire was in his eyes even in the restaurant.

She also knew that she would yield under his touch.

Back in the hotel room he soon had her clothes removed and laid her on the bed. He kissed her and caressed her breasts, touched her between her thighs. Her body instantly responded to his hands, she was defenceless against him, kissing him back, loving him, wanting him.

"Laura, I want you in a different way tonight."

She wasn't sure at first what he meant. She had an idea but it wasn't until he moved his hand to a lower place that she understood. The anxiety showed in her face.

"We'll go really slowly. And only when you're ready," he said.

She trusted him. His went down on her while his finger probed her gently yet firmly. The sensations somehow combined, and although it felt strange and even wrong, his mouth was bringing her near the edge.

He broke off suddenly. "Don't stop," she said.

"I don't want you to come yet. I want you to be absolutely begging for this."

He turned his attention to her breasts and stomach, his mouth making her moan and arch against him, longing for him to touch her where she needed it most, but he wouldn't. Instead he slipped his hand back down to explore her further.

It didn't really hurt but she wasn't sure if she liked it. It made her feel sort of empty because she wanted him inside her, on the front of her. She felt him use two fingers and it was a little painful as he first pushed them into her. He moved his fingers gently inside her. He was stretching her slowly, making sure she would be able to accommodate him.

"Do you want me?" he asked.

She wanted him desperately, but she wasn't sure if she wanted him in the way he did. She was so wet and ready for him, but not there. She felt him using her own wetness to lubricate her ready for him.

"I want to be as close to you as possible. I want to make every part of you mine."

It was his words that she couldn't resist, his possessiveness. It made her want to yield to him.

"What do you want, Laura?"

"I want you." She could barely whisper.

He turned her over and got her to push her knees up underneath her. She was exposed to him from behind, he gripped her wrists as he leant over her so she had no defences. Then she felt him where his fingers had been and he pushed - slowly - persisting even though her body was resisting him.

"Like this? Do you want me here?"

She couldn't answer him. It felt forbidden and she wasn't sure if she wanted him to stop or not. Part of her wanted to be able to give this to him, part of her wasn't sure if he would stop if she asked him to.

"We can take it as slowly as you like," he told her.

Once again it was what he said that scared and thrilled her, and made her resistance slip just enough to let him take her. She felt her body start yielding to him. It did hurt and she couldn't help crying out, and he paused.

"Are you ok? I don't want to hurt you," he said. Letting go of her wrists he stroked her back and kissed down her spine, making her shiver with delight. His hands reached to fondle her breasts. He stayed there for some time.

Then gradually, infinitesimally slowly, he continued to enter her. It took longer than she had thought, but he was gentle, and once he was fully inside her she felt strange and not completely comfortable, but it wasn't terrible.

His touches on the rest of her body were still driving her wild, but he wouldn't touch her where she wanted him to. She tried to move his hand there but he refused, and when she tried to move her own hand there he pushed it away.

"Be patient. We'll get there," he told her.

She was completely in his control. He started to pull back and push again into her, tiny movements. It felt like a dragging followed by more pressure and fullness. After a while he was moving further in and out, still gently but faster.

"I want you to feel me fully, every inch of me. I want you to understand how close I want to be to you, how much I ache for you when I see you every day and can't have you."

Then he finally moved his hand between her legs, just where she wanted it, his fingers finding the exact spot she needed pressure. At the same time he started going faster and harder, but she was distracted from it hurting by his touch elsewhere.

Then as his finger slid over her clit her body started to lose control. It was a deeper, more raw sensation that she had ever experienced with him before. It was darker and she felt it more in her stomach. She also realised she was crying.

She didn't remember much after that. There was a memory of him finally moving from her, wrapping his arms around her and cradling her, but then she must have fallen asleep.

20. Playing away

The next day was a bright jewel in the middle of the long, darkening season. They tried to see as many sights as they could as though they had to cram months of dates into a single day.

This was living in the moment. This was not thinking about the future, or the next week, or even the next day.

Being out in public with him was wonderful. He put his arm around her, they were a couple, in the crowds of anonymous people they didn't have to hide. She felt pride at being with him, several time she saw other girls look at him admiringly.

Laura had a couple of anxious moments when she imagined she saw someone she knew and panicked. But it was just paranoia, they were safe. Most of the time she was able to relax.

"If that really was Pat Ayers coming out of a pub in Soho she'd have more explaining to do than us," Mr Rydell said.

No one seemed to notice their age gap. Laura knew she could look older than her age, she had managed to get into 18 certificate films at the cinema even a couple of years ago. She had tried to make herself look older, getting a new jacket during half term in a more grown up style. She was happy to see several girls in London wearing similar, some of them in their early twenties at least.

Yet there was still the thrill of the forbidden. The times when he would catch her eye and she knew they shared this dangerous secret.

"Sometimes I wonder if we should have waited until you leave school," he said as she had lain in his arms earlier that morning.

"Am I too young for you?"

He silenced her with a kiss, and with his body he again showed her just how perfect she was for him. "You are perfect for me. We fit so well."

Laura felt like she could never get enough of him. Even when he was demanding it was never too much.

But she was worried. Worried that he would get bored of her, or change his mind and look for someone older with more experience. She had nothing to compare anything to, as he was her first lover and first real boyfriend.

She tried to explain this to him, how she was anxious she couldn't meet his needs as much as she wanted him.

"What we did last night, that's not something I need often. Never, if you don't want it. I just needed it one time from you," he told her.

They saw the Crown Jewels and the famous waxworks, then had lunch in Soho before going to the British Museum. At one point they passed a jewellers and he went inside. Coming out he gave her a box.

"This is for you. It's not the Cullinan diamond but you have to have some souvenir."

It was a sparkling stone on a fine gold chain, like a raindrop. Laura loved it and put it on immediately. "I can wear it under my uniform," she said. Jewellery was forbidden at

Francis Hall except for discreet Christian crosses worn below clothing.

She was gladdest of all that they had gone to the British Museum. Something about it moved her, it felt hallowed.

There wasn't enough time to see everything so they picked the most famous artefacts. Laura was imprinting memories: if she ever saw the Elgin Marbles or the Rosetta Stone again she would always remember him.

She liked the Greek and Roman statues best with their smoothly perfect, lifelike marble. Now she had known his body she could look at them and imagine how their muscles would feel beneath her hands. The sculpture she had been making in Art class had transformed after she first slept with him and properly understood how a male torso should feel.

"Charlotte's got us working insanely hard at Latin but I can't make out any of these inscriptions," she said.

He had done Latin A-level and couldn't manage much more than her. "It was a while ago," he said in his defence.

"Last year I couldn't imagine in a million years wanting to do Latin in the Sixth Form, but recently I've been wondering." She had to pick three subjects to focus on next year. Two would definitely be English and History and she had thought of French for the third, but now the idea of doing Latin had come to her.

Thinking about it reminded her of what a long road she had ahead of her still to get to university. Once she was there she would be more his equal, they wouldn't have to hide. But it was a very long way off.

"I would encourage you to do German but I don't suspect I'll be there next year," he said.

She was horrified. "Why not?"

"Because of you. Because of us. It's playing with fire, someone will find out eventually. And I'm not convinced I can trust myself to stop taking risks. I don't want to leave you but for your sake I think it will be safer if I'm not right there."

"You don't want us to see each other anymore? Ever?"

"God no!" he took her hands as they sat on a bench in the Museum. "No as in I definitely do want to see you, all the time in fact. But for the next couple of years it's going to be hard. At least until we can tell your parents about us."

Her initial shock was replaced by a momentary thrill that he wanted to meet her parents. And then the stomach churning reality of how they would react. More in sorrow than anger, she thought. But they would still be furious with him and desperately worried about her.

She wondered if there ever would be a time when she could tell her parents exactly when they had met and when it started. Certainly not for many years. She started imagining the official story she would have to create for them, how she had "bumped into" an old school teacher at university and they had struck up a friendship. He would be well into his thirties then, they might still freak out.

"I was trying to think how I might break it to them. But it can't be now, they wouldn't understand."

"Nor would I in their shoes. If I was your father I would be getting a shotgun."

* * *

Knowing it would be their last night together for a while made them both want to draw it out as long as possible.

He had never made love to her with such tenderness. He moved in and out of her more slowly than usual, staring into her eyes in the semi-darkness.

Streetlights seeped past the edges of the curtain, illuminating the walls. It was impossible to find true darkness in the city.

Afterwards they lay together not wanting to sleep. He ran his finger over her lips, down her throat, over her breasts. "I am learning, studying the shape of your lovely breasts," he said.

"Don't you know them by now?"

"It's Goethe," he told her. "Probably not a text we'll be doing in class."

They had talked in tentative terms about the future, or at least as far as the Christmas holidays. There was one more exeat that term which she could probably spend with him. He also thought they should stop seeing one another during the school week to lower the risk.

"I need to have more self-control when we go back. Otherwise we will get caught."

Probably by Mr Lanaway, Laura thought. It was only a matter of time before he appeared in the art room and the whole game would be up.

Except it wasn't a game. It was the most serious thing she had ever done. It was a choice.

The thought of seeing him nearly every day at school and not being able to talk with him and touch him was agony.

"We'll have to find other distractions. Seeing you in my classroom is not going to be easy."

"I'll miss you if we can't even speak."

"I'll miss you even more but it will be worth the wait. It's only a few weeks to exeat, then the holidays. Imagine just how much I am going to want you after having to wait," he said.

Given how much they craved one another already she could barely imagine it getting any more intense.

PART III

Flying

quare, dum licet, inter nos laetemur amantes:
non satis est ullo tempore longus amor

Let's enjoy being lovers while we can:
Love is never long enough

Sextus Propertius

21. Secret words

Charlotte was bursting to tell them her news: she had managed to sneak out during half term and spend time with Julian. Even more, she had lost her virginity to him. In his car, on the hillside at night, but she was still thrilled about it.

"Three out of four of us now. We'll have to put a harlot warning sign on the dorm door," Susie said.

Julian had even asked Charlotte to stay after Christmas. "Apparently his parents are cool with girlfriends visiting, though we'll have to have separate rooms," she said.

Laura felt envious. It wouldn't be that easy for Mr Rydell and her to stay with one another openly for ages, years even. "How will you get your father to let you go?" she asked.

"I was going to use one of you guys as an excuse. Julian's older brother can pretend to be your dad if my dad rings. His voice is really deep."

"Fine with me," Susie said. "I'll even forge you a letter from my parents if you like, confirming your stay. Don't forget to give me your postal address."

Susie was an adept forger of handwriting though it was of limited use in a boarding school. In a day school you could bring in fake parental notes nearly every day to get out of PE and other disliked activities. At Francis Hall such notes came from Matron or Grace Grant, who would rapidly find out in the staffroom if their authority was being forged.

Margery felt even more lost with Charlotte now joining the ranks of the fallen. She had had a very quiet half term and mainly spent the time doing homework.

"It's my birthday next weekend," Susie announced. "Let's have a midnight feast."

"Just us or the rest of the House?"

"God it would be boring with just the four of us, I was thinking of something a bit less Enid Blyton and ginger beer after lights out. No, we'll get some of the Dunks boys together and kick our heels up. Booze of course, I plan to celebrate in style."

How any part of this was to be achieved was beyond the others. But Susie had it all worked out. Darius had a cousin with a car who would drive them over and the boys would bring the alcohol. "Darius is always sneaking out. His cousin picks him up, they go out on the town and then he sleeps in the car and walks in as normal with the day boys the next day." St Duncan's had day pupils as well as boarders.

"We'll need a venue of course," Susie said. "I was thinking of that pavilion that's not being used."

It was where Laura had first touched Mr Rydell's hand albeit by accident. When she had first really known deep down that she wasn't imagining it all.

"We would all get expelled instantly if anyone found out," Charlotte said.

"It's the thrill isn't it? We'll be fine though."

"Would it just be Julian and Darius?" Laura asked. She was suddenly worried about Jonathan coming. He'd written her an apologetic letter after having to leave her on the night of the sixth form dance, and she'd realised that he still had no idea that it was over between them.

"Have you still not dumped Jonathan?" Susie asked. "He'll be proposing marriage and kids at this rate, blissfully ignorant that you're in love with your German teacher."

Margery had decided she wanted no part of the escapade. The risk it involved made her feel physically sick.

Both Charlotte and Laura also wanted to back out, but they both knew they owed Susie. They would also continue to need her help. Maybe there was some way her plan could be tamed.

* * *

German was agony and ecstasy. Mr Rydell smiled and caught her eye but beyond that had to play things with caution.

She loved being in his presence. Hearing his voice, looking at him. Knowing he was hers, and she was his. Even when she saw Teresa Hubert making her stupid eyes at him she didn't care. She knew he felt the same.

Her fingers found the jewel he had given her through her blouse. She rarely took it off. When she had shown it to the others Susie had informed her it was a diamond. "Look at the box. Shops like that don't sell cubic zirconias."

Laura who loved it regardless had then worried about its value but didn't dare ask. Fortunately Charlotte did so.

"I don't know, probably a grand or so," Susie said. Laura was horrified but Susie seemed quite blithe about the cost.

Charlotte and Laura sat together in the cold Courtyard at break time, the November day grey and chilly. Margery was elsewhere and Susie appeared to have been held back after class by Mrs Ayers again.

"So do you feel different?" Laura asked Charlotte.

"Yes and no. I thought it would seem bigger, like crossing a really major line, but it's just something that's done, isn't it?"

Laura thought about her own situation. She had been changed long before she ever slept with Mr Rydell. Falling in love with him, those early glances, the wondering, that was when her world had changed.

"Are you in love with him? Has he said it?" Laura asked.

"I don't know, and yes. He might have just said it to persuade me though. He didn't need to."

"But you're glad? No regrets?"

Charlotte shook her head. "Why, did you regret it?"

Not for a moment. It had opened up the world for her. "No. I just wanted to make sure you were ok. And that he took care of things, you know."

"Yeah, he did. He was well prepared. I'm going to go on the Pill though. Oh God, there's the Axe. Hide me."

The Geography teacher walked through the Courtyard, freezing everyone in her path. "Imagine how much happier this place would be if she were gone," Charlotte said. "She's a blight."

* * *

Laura was still hanging back to keep pace with Margery in cross country which helped sustain their friendship. Susie had made it into the squad so it was just the two of them which Margery was glad for. She didn't dislike Susie but she found her hard to relate to.

Laura and Margery had also grown closer due to all the extra time Charlotte was spending playing hockey. The combination of hockey and Julian had also quite wiped out Charlotte's good intentions where Latin was concerned.

Margery had been dismayed to find out that Charlotte's original zeal was largely due to one of her Welsh Romeos reading Classics.

"Perhaps it doesn't matter what the motive is if it still leads to a good result," Laura said.

She herself had persisted with putting in extra study for the ancient language. It had made an enormous difference to her grasp and enjoyment of the subject and was the reason she was giving it serious consideration for A-level.

"Will you stay with Mr Rydell for the final exeat?" Margery asked as they passed the groundsman's cottages.

"Probably, if he asks me," Laura said.

"Aren't you worried about getting caught? What if one of the staff dropped round to speak with him?"

"I'd hide upstairs I suppose." Laura hoped it wouldn't happen but it would be kind of exciting if it did.

"Doesn't it bother you always having to sneak around?"

Laura thought about the day in London where she was able to walk around with Mr Rydell openly. "Sometimes."

But it was also thrilling to have a secret that hardly anyone knew about.

* * *

Mr Rydell did manage to communicate with her. When she got her homework back, there was a folded piece of paper inside it.

"I love you and I want you all over again."

He hadn't signed it which meant she could more safely keep it. She tucked it into her journal, its pages left blank since before half term.

Laura wondered if she could send him something back. Then it came to her that she could write something in German in her exercise book. In the unlikely event anyone else ever found it, it would look like homework.

To be on the safe side she decided to choose a quotation. She went to the school library where she found Miss Vine on duty. It had the usual hush that hung thickly in the air over the smell of hardback books.

She found the Modern Languages shelves and pulled out a book of Goethe. This would be tricky as there was no way she could translate it since her German was still too basic a level. So she hunted down an English translation to pick a couple of lines that she could then cross reference in the original German.

Selecting the text was harder than she thought. She didn't want it to be too soppy. Most of the poems were also written from the point of view of a man to a woman. Eventually she found a couplet that she liked, and wrote the German down.

"What bliss it is! We exchange safe kisses,

"Without worry we draw in one another's breath and life."

Instead of "safe" - she wrote *gefährliche* - dangerous.

22. Fooling around

Grace Grant had noticed the endless detentions that the newest pupil was getting. All of them, it would seem, ordered by Mrs Ayers. She was used to the Geography teacher handing out unfair punishment to Michaelmas girls and had argued on their behalf many times, but this was unprecedented. She also noticed that despite doing well in other subjects, Susie's record showed a slew of Cs and Ds for Geography.

She called Susie into her office.

"I notice you seem to be in detention rather frequently for Geography."

"That's right," said Susie.

The housemistress was rather taken aback by her tone. "Is there something the matter?"

"Not that I can think of," Susie said.

Grace Grant could tell there was, but she also recognised that Susie was the type of child who couldn't be prised open by any means. "Perhaps you would let me see your Geography book," she asked.

Susie fetched it, and when Grace Grant opened it she was disturbed. Expecting a messy scrawl of poorly completed work, such as might justify the low grades and repeat punishments, she saw quite the opposite.

Rarely had she seen such carefully done work: neat handwriting, beautifully drawn diagrams, essays that were clearly above and beyond the usual length of an assignment. Geography wasn't her subject, but even a brief read of Susie's work showed it to be quite exceptional. Most worryingly there was a distinct lack of red ink, just a large C, C-, or D scrawled at the end of each entry.

Mrs Ayers was clearly acting towards Susie with sheer vindictiveness, but Grace Grant had no idea why. For the first time in her tenure at the school she felt fear. As she looked at Susie's face, with its polite, impassive expression, she knew that her misgivings were not for Susie.

I shall have to elevate this, she thought. Whatever is going on cannot endure. She had long thought that Mrs Ayers was unhinged, but not to the point of sabotaging a pupil's record.

"Are you concerned about the marks you are getting? Do you feel they are unfair?" she asked her.

"I can only do my best," Susie said.

Whatever game the girl was playing would not end well, for Mrs Ayers and possibly the school as well. It was time to consult Miss Grayson.

* * *

They had vowed to avoid risking further contact outside class but it was Mr Rydell's turn to sit at the head of their table at lunch. It was a more than welcome change from fussy Miss Quayle the previous week.

The others contrived to make sure Laura sat next to him, taking all four places at the top end of the table much to the fury of Teresa Hubert who still fancied her own chances.

Concentrating on normal conversation with his leg pressed against hers under the table was not easy. But she was near him, as near as she could be to him in public, and he could talk directly to her without it drawing undue attention.

"So what are all your plans for the final exeat?" he asked them, knowing full well what Laura's were.

Charlotte had been toying with the idea of "doing a Susie" and spending the exeat hidden in Julian's dorm at St Duncan's. On balance she had decided it was too risky. Susie's birthday escapade would be dangerous enough. Charlotte had just got into the First Eleven hockey team and didn't want anything to jeopardise it. She would instead turn the dullness and constriction of home to her advantage and spend most of the weekend training.

"I'll just be going home. Revising probably." They had exams between the exeat and the Christmas holidays: the last few weeks of term were usually pretty gruelling.

"I'll make sure I prepare you all something sufficiently rigorous in German then," he told Charlotte.

"Please don't. We were hoping you might set us something easy, Sir."

"Harder things are often more interesting." He was pushing his leg more firmly against Laura's as he said this. She reddened but fortunately it seemed to go over everyone else's heads. Those that didn't know what was going on with her and Mr Rydell at least.

"Where are you going for the exeat Sir?" someone asked.

"Staying here, marking your work," he told them. His hand was on Laura's thigh. She was freaking out that someone would see but didn't dare move away lest it made it more obvious.

"Doesn't sound like much fun. You should get out more Sir," Teresa Hubert said, trying to sound flirtatious. Charlotte and Susie caught one another's eye and were trying not to dissolve into laughter.

"Staying in has pleasures of its own." His fingers caressed the inside of Laura's thigh and she jumped, nearly knocking over a glass of water. He looked at her, a gleam in his eye.

"Maybe you should lighten your load and let us off German homework next week," Charlotte said. There was a volley of voices in support of this. "Oh please Sir!" "Go on Sir!"

He smiled. "I'm only happy to sacrifice my holiday to ensure you all excel at German in your end of term exams. Any more requests and I'll set you double."

* * *

Susie was currently absorbed with the midnight feast plans. Her campaign against Mrs Ayers was no longer her primary concern. She had devised her strategy and let it tick along without a great deal of conscious thought.

It was all arranged that Darius and Julian would come over around midnight and meet them by the pavilion. If the gate to the playing fields was padlocked they would scale the railings further along where a tree provided convenient branches. "Don't smash the bottles," she had warned Julian over the phone.

Susie had been in two minds about the guest list. They were taking such a huge risk already that publicising it beyond their dorm would likely be fatal. Someone was bound to let it slip. On the other hand the larger the crowd, surely the lower the chance of a mass expulsion? They might expel her as the ringleader but that didn't worry Susie unduly so long as the others got off with a warning or a few detentions. But she didn't want to drag them all the way down with her.

In the end she decided it would just be the four of them - or the three of them if she couldn't persuade Margery. It might be useful to have Margery snoring in her bed if Matron did make a late round.

"Matron normally sleeps like the biggest log of all. When someone's ill in the night you really have to hammer on her door to get her up," Charlotte said.

Laura desperately wanted Margery to come as otherwise if Darius and Julian brought Jonathan she would end up getting paired up with him. Even if they brought a fourth boy that might help. Would Robert come? That might even persuade Margery to attend. Though if she managed to get off with him Laura was back to her original problem of being one-on-one with Jonathan.

But Margery outright refused.

"I don't care if you all think I'm square. I don't want to mess my entire life up by getting expelled. I wouldn't enjoy it at all, sitting there and stressing over a teacher showing up."

She had a point. Laura wasn't looking forward to it either for much the same reasons.

* * *

His initial attempts to coach Susie privately for the poetry recital rebuffed, Mr Peters had decided to attend the general rehearsals under the guise of lending his assistance to Miss Wingrove. She was forced to tolerate his presence since he was the Head of Department but paid him as little attention as possible.

To Mr Peters' surprise and delight Susie had chosen John Donne's The Flea, replete with its sexual innuendo and imagery. Hearing her recite *"loss of maidenhead"* nearly pushed him over the edge.

"It suck'd me first, and now sucks thee,

"And in this flea our two bloods mingled be."

Susie's recital was quite brilliant and she was only too aware of the ulterior meaning of the lines. Noticing Mr Peters' reaction, Miss Wingrove regretted not having encouraged her to pick a slightly less controversial poem.

"Thank you Susie, that's coming on nicely." She called the next girl up for her practice.

Mr Peters sidled up to Susie.

"That was quite a stunning performance, Susanna. I really felt that you understood Donne's verse, his passion, his sensuality."

Susie had her own plans for Mr Peters though she didn't intend to put them into action just yet. But keeping him on the boil for now - or a light simmer at least - suited her needs.

"I was wondering if I should reference the typographical pun in some way?" she asked him.

The "s" of "suck'd" was printed as "ʃ" in Donne's era resulting in a deliberate visual obscenity.

Mr Peters wet his lips at the thought of Susie uttering such profane words. "If you would like any extra help with your performance I would be only too happy to oblige," he said.

He really was a disgustingly creepy old goat, but she treated him to a suggestive smile.

"I'll let you know Sir."

23. In the night

Grace Grant went to see Mrs Grayson about the situation with Susie and the geography teacher. To her frustration Mrs Grayson was rather dismissive.

"The problem is, Eleanor, that Susie's work is really exemplary. She's also ostensibly very well behaved. The reasons given for all the demerit points and detentions are just absurd."

"You know as well as I do that there are many ways for a pupil to show insolence," the headmistress said.

"I do. I don't disagree that Susie is likely deliberately infuriating Pat Ayers. But these endless detentions aren't fair, and they're not wise."

Mrs Grayson had long known that Mrs Ayers was a problem. She was extremely unpopular with the girls but on the other hand she tended to get excellent results. Two girls had even won places at Cambridge last year following her personal tuition.

While the headmistress thought it was wiser to get results through respect rather than fear, she couldn't deny that Mrs Ayers got them. Personality clashes may have been common but the girls did at least have the option of changing to German if they truly couldn't bear her.

If only Susie had chosen German: but as a new girl she obviously hadn't been forewarned of the Geography teacher's bad temper.

Then of course there were the pranks. Since the foul-smelling curtains rumours of other ones had reached Mrs Grayson's ears. Did the Geography teacher suspect Susie Clarke was behind them?

"I'll keep an eye on things. And have a quiet word with Pat at the right moment," she promised Grace Grant.

* * *

Friday, the eve of Susie's birthday, was bitterly cold. November frost had frozen the grounds and there were biting winds all day with rain setting in after supper. The thought of creeping out of a warm dorm in the middle of such a night to the unheated pavilion had minimal appeal.

"The cold will keep us alert. Besides we can hardly not show up with a carload of Dunks boys arriving," Susie said.

"A carload?"

"I don't know, Darius said they'd bring some people over. He didn't say the number, just as many would fit."

"He'd better be driving a mini then," Charlotte said.

They had already scoped out the pavilion and stashed some provisions there. It was padlocked but there was a window with a faulty latch around the back. There was also no light and no heating.

"We can't use light anyway, it'll have to be something dim like torches or candles. And not many. We don't want to light the place up like a beacon."

"What would someone do if they saw?" Laura asked. "Would they come and investigate or just call the police?"

"Investigate I should think. They wouldn't want the scandal if the police showed up." Charlotte said.

Susie allowed herself a moment's fantasy of Mrs Ayers showing up in a nightgown and overcoat, screeching loud enough to wake the entire school. The instant expulsion would be worth it just to experience that sight. But she had the others to think of. Besides, Whitsun House had no view to the pavilion so unless the Axe was out taking a midnight stroll she would be among the least likely teachers to discover them.

* * *

They had gone to bed in jeans and warm clothing but it was still an ordeal leaving warm blankets for the freezing night air as they crept down the fire escape.

The night had cleared and there was a bright moon. It made the grounds look vast and it raised their spirits. Having successfully escaped Michaelmas House it seemed like the worst hurdle was over. The remoteness of the pavilion was reassuring: they certainly wouldn't be overheard.

Breathless from the cold they clambered through the window into the dark building. Charlotte lit a candle.

"Make sure you put it in a jar, we don't want to burn the place down. Oh I can see them coming," Susie said.

"How many?"

"Five it seems. I don't recognise the others."

To Laura's relief the other three boys didn't include Jonathan. They were three more St Duncan's rugby players, very much in the mould of Julian and Darius, and had hauled an impressive amount of beer with them. They already seemed fairly drunk.

The discussion soon got onto gambling as Susie's win over the previous exeat had become the stuff of legend. There were jibes over whether it was luck or cheating and demands for the chance to win it back.

The noise level was increasing with the alcohol. Susie was the only one of the three girls really enjoying herself. Laura and Charlotte were still too on edge. Laura constantly thought she heard footsteps outside.

"It's just an owl or something," Julian said.

Darius had brought playing cards with him and by the dim candlelight the five St Duncan's boys started a game with Susie. As the other two didn't know how to play they sat and watched.

It was the poker game that saved all their skins.

Conversation lulled to near silence as the players focused on the hands, both Darius and Julian determined to win back their pride and Susie resolute in repeating her success.

"Anybody in there?"

There was a loud rattle at the door. In the stillness of the night it was like gunshot.

It was Jenkins, the school handyman.

Oh God.

Sheer, raw panic.

Everyone froze.

Darius snuffed the candle. Charlotte gripped Laura's hand in terror.

"Hello? Who's in there?"

Jenkins obviously hadn't got the key to the padlock. The front windows which looked across the fields were shuttered so he couldn't see in from that side at least. They heard him walk around the building to the back windows.

The stillness. The terror.

Eight of them stuck in the freezing darkness of the wooden building facing exposure at any moment.

The broken window wasn't shuttered but it was closed, and it was a smaller window than the front ones. The moon was also shining on the front ones rather than the back. If they remained in the shadows, completely still, and Jenkins couldn't see in clearly then perhaps, perhaps he wouldn't see them.

Except the smoke. The damn cigarette smoke. It must reek in the night air, Laura thought. Would he have a torch with him?

She closed her eyes; it was actually hard to breathe properly. The fear in the room was sobering. They had felt invincible but the reality was instant expulsion if they were discovered: catastrophic for the St Duncan's Sixth formers who were mid-way through university applications.

The eight of them waited for several minutes. Jenkins had gone past the window and round to the front again, rattling the door one more time.

"If there's anyone in there I'm calling the police."

Then there was silence.

Cat-like, Susie made her way to the front windows and managed to peer through a tiny chink where the wooden shutter had warped.

"He's gone. He's half way back to the gate."

Laura felt like crying. There were plenty of oaths under people's breath.

"We'll have to get out quickly, he might come back with reinforcements," Julian said.

"And the key."

One by one they clambered out of the window as quickly and quietly as they could. Darius and Julian passed the remainders of the feast through, mainly empty bottles and crisps.

"Hold on," said Susie. "Someone has to piss in there."

"What?" Charlotte looked at her as though she was mad.

"Jenkins knows there was someone in here. They'll be over this place with a toothcomb first thing tomorrow, probably with the police too. We need to make them think it's a tramp."

She grabbed an old rug from the pavilion that they'd been sitting on, and trampled it into the mud below the window. Then she poured some beer dregs on it and tossed it back into the room. "That's his bed. Now throw in a couple of fag ends and one - no two - empty bottles. Now one of you boys go in and do the business."

At a nod from Julian one of the three rugby players went back in. They all waited for him.

"In the corner and a bit on the blanket. Let's hope that does it," he reported on exit.

"Short of throwing a battered old hat and a spotted kerchief on a stick to completely over-egg the pudding, I should think we're done," Darius said.

Laura was simply horrified by the whole situation. It was bad enough to sneak out but to foul the place up was unbearably wrong.

She wasn't even aware, nor did she really care, how the boys got back to the gate. She, Charlotte and Susie hurried off back to Michaelmas House trying to keep to the shadows as far as possible. They took their shoes off at the bottom of the fire escape to climb up with minimum noise. They crept into the dorm where Margery was gently snoring and slid into their beds, fully clothed.

Everything was flashing in Laura's mind when she tried to sleep. She kept imagining the worst scenarios. And what was Mr Rydell going to say if she got expelled? She hadn't been able to tell him about the party as they hadn't spoken alone since half term

How she wished she could be with him now: safe, holding her, soothing away the fear.

24. Covering tracks

They were disarmed the next morning by a surprisingly sincere apology from Susie. "I should never have dragged you guys into it, it was totally unfair. I know you didn't really like the idea. I thought I had it all sorted and I didn't. Actually that's not quite true, I knew it was a huge risk which was part of the fun, but it was totally unfair to put that on you."

"It's ok, we agreed to come and it was your birthday. You don't owe us an apology," Charlotte said.

"I do. And the tramp thing, it's foul to have done that on school property. I never meant that to happen but I was running out of ideas."

Laura had woken up that morning feel less revulsed and more relieved by Susie's strategy. "I think it was smart, actually. Otherwise they would start sniffing around and the pressure might get too much."

They all knew she meant Margery. Not that Margery would tell directly, but she might give the game away by her reaction to any questioning.

"Who ended up winning by the way?" Charlotte asked.

"I was ahead by a mile, more's the pity. The boys will be toasting old Jenkins for years to come."

"We'll look on this one day and laugh," Laura said. "Happy birthday by the way."

"Thanks. It will be a happy one if we continue to get away with this," Susie said.

Charlotte looked at Laura anxiously. "Will you tell Mr Rydell?"

It was something Laura had been uncertain about. She had had so little time to speak with him since half term and Susie's plan had been so last minute.

"I'll probably mention it, but not every detail."

"He won't tell will he? He might feel obligated." Charlotte was worried.

"Of course he won't tell. If he felt some overwhelming moral duty to report misbehaviour he'd start with himself. Keeping quiet about an illicit party pales in comparison to screwing one of your pupils, doesn't it?" Susie said.

Laura felt conflicted. She realised that it could compromise him to tell him certain things. He still had his duties as a teacher and it was dangerous enough for him to be in a relationship with her. She couldn't make him complicit in their rule-breaking as well.

"You know thinking about it I don't think I'll say anything. Not now anyway. Maybe ages later in the future when it really doesn't matter anymore," she said.

After all, he must have secrets he didn't tell her. He must hear things about her friends from other teachers, or know things that he didn't burden her with. Ultimately it was Susie's secret: her birthday, her idea, and she who had done her best to save them all from disaster.

* * *

Susie was in two minds about attending detention that day. It was her birthday after all, and spending valuable leisure hours cooped up yet again did not seem appealing or fair. She knew that the flawless work in her Geography exercise book was a growing gun.

The end of term exams were also going to be interesting. She would easily top the class by a mile if Mrs Ayers marked her fairly. Susie was certain however she would not. But a wrongly marked exam paper would be in a very different league from a spiteful C on a homework essay.

Susie wondered what Mrs Ayers' defence would be if that happened. Would they just let her get away with it? Put it down to an unfortunate error of judgement? She was aware how little weight she carried against a teacher of many years - decades - who must have some value to Francis Hall if she had lasted so long with such a malevolent personality.

To Susie's delight Teresa Hubert was also in detention that week. Teresa had been caught copying answers in Maths. Which wasn't stupid in itself, everyone did it from time to time, but it was immensely stupid when the person she copied from, Andrea, had even more miserable mathematical abilities than Teresa's. Identical wrong answers were an obvious giveaway. Of course if Teresa was less stupid, Susie thought, she would have copied them from Mary Rudge or someone who was good at Maths.

"What are you in for?" she asked Teresa, knowing full well what the answer was.

"A misunderstanding," Teresa said.

"A little misunderstanding in Maths?" Susie asked with a falsely polite smile. Teresa scowled at her.

"Why are you here?" As Teresa did German and not Geography, she knew nothing of Susie's feud with Mrs Ayers.

"Sheer pleasure," Susie said.

It turned out to be closer to Her Majesty's Pleasure that afternoon, since detention was taken by Mrs Grayson. Although the Headmistress was liked and respected, unlike teachers such as Mrs Ayers and Miss Quayle, no one dared breathe out of line when she presided over an event. Susie's racy novel would have to stay out of sight today.

Mrs Grayson's patience had already been tried that morning by Jenkins and his absurd and alarming account of a tramp invading the pavilion. The police had been round to investigate but found nothing much. It seemed a window had been forced.

"Stinking mess it was too, not as I like to say it out loud but he'd used it as a facility so to speak," Jenkins had said.

Jenkins had been instructed to clean the room and fix the window as well as check various other windows and locks around the school as a priority, but Mrs Grayson remained troubled. A vagrant breaking into a girls' school might have more sinister motives than shelter for the night. She needed to put the school on higher caution without creating alarm. Schoolgirls were prone to drama and she didn't want to make mountain out of a molehill and trigger a slew of false alerts and mass panic.

Yet she was troubled. Something seemed wrong with the school that term but she hadn't been able to pinpoint what it was. There was the disruption from Miss Vine's plan with the school play of course. Yet nothing untoward had arisen from that so far beyond a few friendships developing between pupils of the two schools. Mrs Grayson was of the mind that these things would happen anyway among young people - just look at Romeo and Juliet - so it wasn't a major concern. Better, all things said and done, to know what was going on. She didn't want another Lucy Martin on her hands.

She looked at the dark head of the new pupil on the back row, seemingly intent on her work. Of course Susie Clarke wasn't the only new pupil that term, there was an entire intake of new girls in the youngest class. But she was the only new girl in her year.

She remembered what Grace Grant had said to her about Susie's endless detentions. Looking at her now the phrase "butter wouldn't melt" came to mind but Mrs Grayson had been a schoolmistress far too long to take anything at face value.

Going over to Susie's desk to see what she was working on the Headmistress noticed a birthday badge pinned on her jersey. Badges weren't strictly allowed but an exception was usually made for birthdays.

"Is it your birthday today, Susie?" Susie said it was. "A very happy birthday then. I should have thought you would have taken more care to stay out of detention to celebrate your day."

Susie saw Teresa Hubert smirking but was unfazed. "Yes, is it unfortunate," she told the Headmistress.

It wasn't the response she would have expected from most girls but looking at Susie, cool and composed, Mrs Grayson felt some of the reservations that Grace Grant had had. It was to be expected, perhaps, that given Susie's near-expulsions from other schools she wouldn't be the most ordinary or most easy girl. But whereas defiance or disobedience might have been anticipated from such a case, this was something else.

It needed some careful thought. The Headmistress determined to speak with Grace Grant again, and meanwhile make her own observations of Susie.

* * *

Mr Poynter had asked some of his history class to volunteer to help mend old books in the library on Saturday afternoon. He used Mars Bars as a bribe but those that signed up to help actually did so because they liked him. The weather was awful anyway and there were no other activities planned that weekend.

Susie of course had detention, Charlotte had hockey and Margery wanted to do some homework so Laura was the only one of the four to volunteer.

Mr Poynter started referring to it as the Bookbinding Club and Laura hoped with a heavy heart that it wouldn't become a too-frequent event. As school societies went it would rank below even the prayer circle and the knitting group in terms of social cachet.

Feeling fairly ambivalent but with nothing better to do she made her way to the library. She walked by herself as the other girls taking part were from different houses.

As she crossed into the main school buildings Mr Rydell came up beside her. "Heading anywhere interesting?" he asked. He was still wearing his work clothes. Teachers rarely ever wore casual clothes around the school even if they were off duty.

It was thrilling to get a brief moment with him alone. "Only the library," she said. "Mr Poynter wants us to help him mend some old books. He bribed us with chocolate and a future school excursion."

"That's where I'm going too. Though Charles - Mr Poynter - roped me in with the promise of some beer."

As she walked next to him - this tall, athletic, good looking man - Laura wished the whole world could know that she was with him, that he was hers. They passed Miss Quayle and Miss Vine in the courtyard and she wondered what they would think if they knew. They were his colleagues, on the same level as him, and she was just a pupil. Yet she was the one closest to him, with the most intimate knowledge of him. It gave her a strange pride when she thought about it.

They had reached the library steps and he ushered her in first.

"It's not quite what I would plan for a date but if it gets me an afternoon with you, Mr Poynter has my every thanks," he said.

The History teacher was delighted to see them all. "Welcome, welcome. Great to see so many dedicated book lovers."

It was easy to contrive to sit next to one another at one of the shared tables. As they got to work with tape, scissors and the various bookbinding materials he could press his leg against hers. Just being in physical contact with him was wonderful.

Being in the library also gave them a green light to talk in low voices.

"How has your week been?" he asked.

She couldn't answer this truthfully without mentioning the midnight feast which she had decided not to tell him about for now, least of all at a time like this.

"Lessons pretty much as usual," she said. She hated having a lie between them, or an absence of truth, and for a moment felt badly towards Susie for putting her in such a position. But if it wasn't for Susie hardly any of her time with him would have been possible, in fact the whole thing might never have happened if Susie's advice hadn't helped Laura pluck up her courage.

So on balance, Susie had helped her. And Laura more than owed it to her to keep silent about the party. Put like that, as a debt to Susie rather than a lie to Mr Rydell, it didn't seem so bad.

"None of the others joining you today?" He referred to her dorm mates.

"All busy. Susie has yet another detention. Mrs Ayers again."

"That woman is a blight," he said. He spoke so low that no one could hear him except Laura.

"That's exactly what Charlotte says," she told him.

"The way I saw her treat you after you had fallen that time, I felt violent with anger. Even if it hadn't been you I would have been furious."

"Did you already know by then how you felt? About me?"

"I knew from the start. I couldn't get you out of my mind. When I called you back to my classroom I was tempted to make a move even then," he said.

"I wanted you to."

He linked his foot around her ankle. "I want you right now. Isn't there some dark corner or long lost book vault we can find?"

"No, only upstairs and it's always busy." The upper level of the library was reached by a spiral staircase. Anyone could go up there to get a book, but only Sixth Formers were allowed to work on the desks up there. It didn't look as though anyone was up there currently, but you couldn't see the whole area from where they were sitting.

"Let's try it."

"Are you serious? What will Mr Poynter say?"

He ignored her protests. "What books are up there?"

"English literature."

Mr Rydell got up, and spoke in a deliberately louder voice. "You can show me where they are, Laura. Charles, there are some very dog-eared poets that have apparently escaped attention. Practically falling apart." Mr Poynter had naturally focused most of the initial efforts on preserving the works of his own subject, History.

"We should do those as a priority," Mr Poynter agreed.

Mr Rydell went up the stairway, getting Laura to follow him. They were in luck: there were no Upper School girls working up there that afternoon.

In an instant he had pulled her to the side of the upper level that was out of view of those below. He pushed her back against the shelves and pinning her there, kissed her. She smelt his skin, drank in his male scent, felt the roughness of stubble against her face.

His tongue explored her while he moved her hand onto his groin. He was rock hard. "It's not easy to stick books together with that distracting me," he said.

Laura had never felt so turned on. She wanted that hardness, wanted to bring him relief, wanted to bring herself relief. The fleeting moments that they could allow themselves to embrace, the presence of the others below, the intensity of their desire and the massive risk: it was insanity. It was also the sexiest thing in the world.

"God knows how I'm going to wait until Exeat," he said, breaking away. "Or find these supposed crumbling literary texts that we've promised Mr Poynter." Swiftly he grabbed an old copy of Spenser and pulled a couple of pages loose. "Always found him overrated, but we'll fix him up better than ever before." He grabbed a couple of other books that did look in need of repair and they went back down the stairs.

25. Private lessons

After never being properly alone with Mr Rydell since half term, except for the brief moment in the library, by exeat Laura felt she would burst. The nights had drawn in for winter so it was already dark when she slipped off to the groundsman's cottages again. She had borrowed Charlotte's coat as it had a hood.

Having been pent up for weeks he did not let her off lightly.

They lay in bed, Laura exhausted but completely happy, talking together about various things when he stopped her.

"Did you just call me Sir?"

She was mortified. They were so used to calling the male teachers by this title that it had just slipped out with him. Possibly because she had made more of a conscious effort to use it in German lessons to mask any sense of familiarity. She started to apologise.

"Don't apologise, I think I rather like it," he told her.

She wasn't sure if he was joking. Then he moved her hand onto him. He was rock hard.

"Already?" She was surprised as he never usually recovered this quickly.

"You saying that did it. You'd better say it again."

"How?" She wasn't sure what he wanted.

"Ask me to fuck you."

She found it hard to say things like this though she knew it turned him on. And it turned her on too, being made to say them.

"Please fuck me Sir."

"Say it again," he ordered.

She complied and he grabbed her and took possession of her. She was slightly bruised from his forcefulness before but he didn't go any more gently on her. "Keep saying it," he ordered.

"I want you to fuck me Sir." She looked directly at him while she said it. It was the first time they had directly played off the power imbalance between them, any sense of equality gone. She was his pupil and his subordinate and he was fully in charge.

He was done in seconds, the fastest ever. Then he went down on her and brought her to liquid in less than a minute. She was amazed how quickly he got her there.

"For God's sake never call me that in class again. I'll get flashbacks," he said.

She looked up at him, into his eyes. "I love you Sir." She was half mocking him, half meaning it. She saw the effect that it had on him, his eyes darkening.

"Stop, I can't go again, it will be physically painful," he said.

She knew now that she could say it whenever she wanted to get leverage. Wrap him around her little finger. How strange that submitting - or playing at submitting - actually gave her more power over him.

* * *

True to his word he started coaching her in English even though she pointed out that university entrance was ages away.

"If you get a handle on this now, you'll coast it later on. I want to give you some advantage if I can."

When he went through the texts and her work with her he switched back into teacher mode. It was different from English lessons because it was one-on-one, so she was getting more individual attention in a single session than she would get from a term with Mr Peters.

He took the tuition seriously which Laura found disconcerting at first, expecting him to play around with her. She hadn't expected him to just do her homework for her but she had thought it might be a more leisurely experience.

But he was equally as good a teacher of English literature as he was of German, so she soon became absorbed as well.

"This is really to A-level standard, this degree of criticism and analysis," he said. "But it's worthwhile getting a grasp of it now."

He introduced a lot of background material and context: texts which she had occasionally heard of but hadn't ever studied. She started to understand how these earlier works, as well as the historical context, illuminated the texts they were doing. In fairness to Mr Peters he had also referenced some of this material but only fleetingly. Teaching a class of a couple of dozen pupils couldn't compare to solo tuition.

Mr Rydell worked with her for over an hour, breaking apart her latest essay and showing her how she could have structured it better and what else she could have included.

"I wish you could help transform my Maths like this. Or Physics."

He smiled. "You probably know more calculus than I do. Six weeks after taking my final exam it was wiped from my mind."

As he turned back to the texts, Laura wound her leg through his and leaned against him.

"That's going to distract me if you do that."

"Maybe I should do this in class?" she said.

Laura wanted to make the most of her time with him, homework could wait. She turned more fully towards him, moving over his lap so she was straddling him. She kissed his lips feeling him draw in his breath. But before he could respond and deepen the kiss she moved to his cheek, then down his neck, loving the rasp of his stubble. He was so utterly male.

She unbuttoned his shirt. She never got to do this because he was usually first to tear her clothes off, shedding his own rapidly before she even got a chance. This time he let her. She ran her hands over his chest, feeling his muscles and the heat of his skin as she moved them round to his back.

He was so broad she had to be close against him to reach fully around him. His hands were already caressing her own back but he held off from undressing her.

"You can continue the lesson," she said.

Then shifting back slightly so she could access his belt, she undid him and moved his boxers aside, allowing his hardness to spring up. Holding gently with both hands she put her mouth around it, feeling the soft, hot, velvety head.

He swore, suppressing a groan as she swirled her tongue around him.

Laura wasn't sure how deep she could take him but she wanted him to know how much she desired him. She tried as far as possible but he was so huge.

He didn't seem to care, just from what she was doing she had felt him grow even harder, hearing his breathing grow ragged.

Now she moved her hands over his thighs and between them, feeling the tautness of him, the fullness, how ready he was to burst.

"If you keep touching me there I'll lose it," he warned.

That made her want to touch him all the more but she also wanted to draw this out. She wanted to make him wait like he so often forced her to wait.

She broke off from what she was doing and raised her head to look up at him.

"Oh god don't stop," he said.

Smiling, she bent her head back down and very slowly moved her lips over him again. He twitched as she did so and she heard him catch his breath in his throat. She loved the feeling of power she had over him, it made her throb between her own legs.

Slowly - infinitesimally slowly - she lowered her head and took him in deeper. She swirled her tongue around and at the same time cupped him, applying gentle pressure just where he had warned her not to.

She could tell from his breathing he was about to lose it so she kept up what she was doing. Then suddenly he gave a jerk and pulled out of her, and it started going everywhere, some against her face. He was gripping her shoulders, his eyes had been closed but he opened them and saw.

"Christ..." It seemed to make him come even longer, he closed his eyes again and she thought he would never stop spasming.

"You could have stayed there," she said when he had finally finished and was recovering.

"I didn't know if you wanted me to. Did you want me to?"

She nodded.

"Next time then." His traces were drying on her skin. "You have no idea how much it turns me on to see you like that."

"Sticky and messy." She smiled seductively at him.

"Marked as mine."

Later they came as near as they ever had done to arguing when she tried to get him to change his mind about looking for another job. The prospect of seeing him barely once a term, if she could even get away at half term, was unbearable.

"Laura if you were ten years older, even five, I would ask you to marry me. But I'm not going to do that to you now, even if we could run off to Gretna Green. It wouldn't be fair on you."

"But what if I wanted it too?" She knew that she never wanted to be without him.

"You might want it now, but who knows if you would feel the same in a few years? You need to be able to live your life, go to university, make your own choices without being tied down," he said.

"You might change your mind too."

"It's easier to know what I want with a few more years of life experience under my belt. This kind of thing... it doesn't come along twice in a lifetime. Not for me anyway. But it might for you."

"So you want to break up with me?"

"I never want to lose you, I never want to stop seeing you. But as selfish as I want to be, I'm not going to stand in your way. If in a few years time you feel the same then we can have a different conversation. But right now we just have us, today. Let's not think about the future for now."

Yet she felt that now was running out of time. She wanted a tomorrow. A forever.

* * *

Teresa Hubert knew what she had seen. Or she thought she did. Her parents had been late picking her up for exeat and she had been waiting in the common room, with its views over the playing fields, when she saw a figure in the distance walking along the path to the groundsman's cottages.

Even though it was dark there was enough illumination from nearby streetlights for Teresa to recognise the coat instantly. It was Charlotte's. No one else in Michaelmas House had one with such a distinctive hood. But the figure didn't look tall enough to be Charlotte and besides she was certain she'd seen Charlotte's father's car earlier.

She watched as the person was let into the cottage but from the angle, the distance and the darkness she couldn't tell who it was.

It had to be one of the others in Charlotte's dorm. What were they doing visiting Mr Rydell after dark on a Friday evening?

Whoever had gone there didn't emerge and Teresa was waiting there for at least half an hour according to her watch.

It must be Susie, Laura or Margery. Margery she ruled out immediately because there was no way she would be visiting a man at night. She just wasn't the type. Unless it was for some kind of extra German tuition? That would admittedly be more like Margery. It would be easy to rule Margery out, she could call her bluff and Margery would cave immediately.

Teresa considered Susie to the most likely in terms of character. She thought Susie was a slut, partly because she was jealous of her. Susie was extremely pretty and the rumours that she was seeing Darius Iles, one of the elite set of St Duncan's, had riled Teresa. Who did she think she was coming here and immediately taking up with a boy like that?

But Susie didn't do German so how could she possibly know Mr Rydell well enough to visit him at his home?

That left Laura. Teresa wasn't particularly observant in class because she was full of her own self importance and liked to fancy that Mr Rydell had a special fondness for her. She certainly couldn't recall anything that would suggest Laura knew him better than anyone else.

Teresa didn't like Laura but she didn't hate her as much as she hated Charlotte. But they came as a set, those four, and despite what Teresa thought of as her kindnesses to Margery she still didn't feel that she had made any progress with her affection.

She brooded about it all weekend. By Sunday night she had decided to report what she had seen. It would be interesting to stir the pot, and hopefully one of them would be in for it. But first she would see if she could get anything out of Margery. She must know something, they were all as thick as thieves.

26. Exposure alert

Margery was in the common room doing some extra study. She couldn't think of much else to do these days. Since the midnight feast the others had been closer than ever. She didn't regret not going but she regretted the growing distance between her and the others. Even throwing herself into her studies didn't really fill the gap.

It was here that Teresa Hubert found her sitting by the long windows that overlooked the playing fields. The same place that Teresa had seen what she had seen.

"Catching up on homework? All work and no play," she said.

This stung. Margery might have been fertile soil for Teresa's scheming, but the idle remark triggered Margery's bristles. Someone else had jokingly called Margery a swot that week and it had made her sensitive about her studies versus her social life.

"She's an interesting girl, Susie Clarke, isn't she?" Teresa began.

Given Teresa had frequently referred to Susie as a slag and a tart, Margery knew something nasty was up.

"Of course I realise she's from a different background to us, but I'm not sure that her parents would like her going visiting men late at night, do you?"

Margery said nothing. Had Teresa found out about the midnight feast? Had she spotted Susie with Darius somewhere?

"That's if it was Susie. I know it was one of you, because who else would borrow Charlotte's coat. Perhaps it was you, Margie?"

"What are you talking about?" Margery finally rose to the bait. She was genuinely in the dark about what Teresa was digging at.

"Whichever of you visited the groundsman's cottages late on Friday night before the exeat, for an interestingly long time."

Margery was silent. All her life she would remember this moment: the stillness, the smell of the room and the books and the floorboards covered with a worn rug, the scent of the threat.

"It wasn't Charlotte, because I saw her leave. So it must have been Susie, you or Laura. But you're not that kind of girl are you are Margie? We're not cheap like that, are we?" Teresa tried a final lunge to get Margery on side.

"I have no idea what you're going on about," Margery said.

"Well then it must have been one of the other two. Perhaps Gi-Gi will be able to work out whom. I'll have to tell her of course, because it's not right is it? Pupils fraternising with teachers. I'm sure your father would agree."

Margery thought that she had never loathed anyone quite so much as she loathed Teresa Hubert at that moment. Or feared, perhaps. But she had enough sense and courage not to react.

Teresa left with one of her unpleasant smiles.

* * *

There wasn't much time to lose. Margery knew that Grace Grant wasn't currently in Michaelmas House which might at least buy them some time. Teresa likely wouldn't go straight to her anyway. She would probably wait a little while to see if Margery would crack, or approach the others. After all Teresa clearly didn't yet know the full extent of what she wanted to know.

Charlotte was currently at hockey practice. Laura was somewhere over in the main school rehearsing for Miss Wingrove's recital. Margery raced to the dorm where she was gladder to find Susie than she would have ever thought possible. It was only four flights of stairs but she was completely out of breath.

"Teresa. Knows."

"What's wrong?" asked Susie, alarmed.

"It's Teresa. Saw. Going to tell."

Susie managed to get Margery to sit down and get her breath back. Gradually Margery calmed down and Susie managed to unravel the story.

Susie had the kind of mind that worked like lightning under pressure. She immediately recognised that the game would be up and the fallout catastrophic if the truth came out.

"You wait here, Margie. I'll deal with this. You just continue to know nothing. It'll all be ok."

Margery was crying. "It will ruin Laura's life! I knew this was a mistake, I told you all so. She'll be expelled and her future will be ruined!"

"Get a grip. Just stay up here, out of Teresa Hubert's way. Read a book or something. You did really well not to let her pump you. I promise you I'll fix this. There is always a way."

She already knew what the way was going to be, but coordinating the others would be the biggest challenge. Let alone convincing them.

* * *

Susie had staked out Grace Grant's study for the past hour. Fortunately there was no sign of Teresa Hubert. Susie hoped she hadn't gone to try and confront Laura, whom she didn't trust not to cave.

Finally the housemistress arrived, and Susie took her chance.

"I need to see you urgently Miss Grant." They always called her Miss Grant to her face even though she was a widow.

"Come in then, Susie."

Grace Grant's study was a tranquil room on the side of the House. The windows looked onto a small garden backed by bushes outside, rather than the wide expanse of the hockey pitches. The garden was dull and flowerless at this time of year but there was still plenty of foliage.

Susie began. "I've done something really stupid. I've been feeling bad about it for days but I was too embarrassed to say anything."

"If you're here in one piece it can't be the end of the world," the housemistress said.

"It's very bad and I expect I'll have to be expelled," Susie said. She was hedging her bets that her story wouldn't merit expulsion and that to follow this with an anticlimax would soften it further.

"Go on."

Susie had been wondering how to play this. A lot depended on Grace Grant's perception of her. Would she be more convinced if Susie was contrite but a little brazen, or contrite and collapsing in sobs? She decided the former. The housemistress wasn't that stupid, though Susie anticipated that tears might be needed further along.

"I had this thing in my head about an older man, you know. So I sort of had this crush. And I know it's really foolish and inappropriate but I got carried away. So I went and sort of flung myself at him."

"Was this something that happened at half-term, Susie?" Grace Grant asked.

"No, it was here in school." She saw the housemistress's eyebrows raised. "And it was a huge mistake and I really regret it but one of the other girls has been having a go at me about it so I thought I should come clean."

"What exactly happened?"

"I sort of... tried to proposition Mr Rydell." Susie had worked herself into her part so well that she actually managed to blush at this point. Meanwhile her brain was working furiously to visualise how he might genuinely have reacted in such a situation.

Grace Grant had experienced many things in her years of teaching but this threw her. Susie wasn't even in the Upper School yet. She knew the girl was precocious but this was bizarre behaviour.

"I imagine he didn't respond how you intended." She hoped against hope that the German teacher hadn't responded how Susie intended.

"No he was very shocked and embarrassed. I think he was quite angry but he tried to be kind. He made me feel such a moron." Susie was getting into the swing of this now. In her own mind it had practically happened for real. "He made me a cup of tea because I was in a state and then told me to go back to the House." She knew the tea thing was pushing it but she had to account for the length of time that Teresa claimed to have observed.

It was time for Grace Grant to pass judgement.

"This was a very serious and silly thing to do Susie. I realise you might like to think of yourself as sophisticated, but you are only a schoolgirl and you have your whole life ahead of you to experience boys and relationships. This kind of foolishness could not only ruin your own life but could have ruined Mr Rydell's reputation and career as well. I appreciate that you regret what you have done, but you must realise how badly it could compromise him."

Susie attempted what she believed was meant by "hanging one's head".

"Should I write to him and apologise?"

"I don't think that will be appropriate or necessary. I will have a private talk with him and if you can give me your word of honour that you won't attempt anything like this again, we may be able to put this all behind us."

Grace Grant was very unsettled. She needed more time to think about the matter. Something, she felt, wasn't right. Had she seen the gleam of relief and triumph in Susie's eyes she would have had even graver doubts.

* * *

A mammoth task lay ahead with very little time. Susie had to get to Laura to warn her to keep her mouth shut. She had to get to Mr Rydell to convince him to let her take the bullet for them. And she had to get to Teresa Hubert to let her know her plan was foiled. That last would at least be a pleasure.

She couldn't manage all three in the time available. In particular she could hardly track Mr Rydell down now herself for a private rendezvous. Charlotte would need to take on that task. Hopefully she would be finished with hockey practice by now. Susie went to the changing rooms to set up an ambush.

On the way she had the misfortune to bump into Mr Peters.

"Susanna! Headed to the library, I see?" Her route to the changing room took her in the same direction.

"Actually I have to fetch some gym kit."

"And how is your recital progressing? Don't forget my offer to help in any way I can. The Metaphysical poets have long been a special area of interest of mine." He gave her what he felt was a warm and suggestive smile. To Susie it looked more like a leer.

"There are a couple of lines I'm getting stuck on," Susie said. This was a lie.

"Never hesitate to ask if you need assistance. It's always a delight to teach a truly receptive mind."

Fortunately they had reached the changing room. She escaped into its stale sweat, body spray and muddy-shoe scented sanctuary.

27. Cover up

Laura was white with shock and looked close to vomiting. Susie had managed to get her to the music rooms so they could talk as privately as possible.

"It's all ok. Gi-Gi lapped it up. It all hangs on you and Mr Rydell now, just don't do anything idiotic. Remember it's worse for me, not better, if you now go and confess. As it is I've got away with it all pretty much. If she finds out I was lying we're all for the chop. The others may get dragged in too."

"I have to see him."

"No you absolutely don't. Not now, no way. Charlotte is handling it. If you love him for God's sake don't wreck this for him."

* * *

Charlotte played her part admirably after Susie had cornered her in the changing room and explained the crisis. Buoyed by a very successful practice Charlotte was still on a high when she tracked down Mr Rydell. By a stroke of luck he was in the German classroom with no one else around.

He initially reacted exactly as Susie had predicted to Charlotte that he would. He was utterly opposed to Susie taking the fall and it took all of Charlotte's persuasion to convince him.

"If you don't go along with this, we're all fucked. Particularly you and Laura. Susie knows what she's doing, I know you don't teach her so you don't really know her, but she's not like other girls," Charlotte said.

"I'm becoming increasingly aware of that," he said. "But I can't let her lie for me."

"She's not doing this for you. We're doing this for Laura, she's our friend."

"I need to think about this."

"There's no point three people going down when no one needs to. Susie's done this now. Don't screw it up by being noble, she won't thank you," Charlotte said.

He ran his hands through his hair. He looked exhausted.

"You'd better run along. Tell Laura…" He broke off, not knowing what message it was appropriate to send via Charlotte, if any. He didn't want her to be compromised any more than she already was.

But they were all, as Susie had put it, in it up to their necks.

Charlotte could see that the battle was won. "Tell her what?"

"Tell her that everything will be OK."

"That's it?"

He looked directly at Charlotte, his grey eyes meeting hers. For a moment she saw him as Laura saw him and understood everything better than she had done before. He was a person first, their German teacher second. Mr Rydell was flawed in terms of how he had yielded to temptation and crossed the line. But he genuinely loved Laura. Charlotte grew up in that moment, recognising something she hadn't understood before. In a way it temporarily reversed their roles. She was the one in command of the situation.

"I'll tell her you love her, and that she needs to be patient."

His eyes expressed gratitude and relief.

"Thank you."

* * *

It was the elephant in the room. The thing that none of them dared discuss. It was hardest for Laura because she had never needed so much to talk with the others about it, particularly Susie, but none of them felt safe even holding a conversation about it for now.

Susie had seen off Teresa Hubert effectively, or so she hoped. "Margie told me that you've been stirring. I hate to take the wind out of your sails but I've already been to see Gi-Gi and told her all there is to tell. Which is nothing - I paid him a brief visit, no more. So feel free to go and tell your sneaky tales but it won't be news to her."

Teresa was livid but she knew when she was beaten. She suspected that whatever Susie had told the housemistress contained a multitude of lies but she had no additional proof of anything herself. Doubtless Susie had come up with some excuse for what was likely a liaison of the worst sort.

Teresa was convinced that someone like Susie was the kind of girl to act in the most promiscuous way possible. But the wrath of Mr Rydell was another consideration. If she wrongly accused them of having an affair he would be incandescent with rage and despise her forever. Even if she rightly accused them he would be furious.

Then there was her own crush on the German teacher. It was more comforting to hope that Susie might have been telling the truth that nothing was going on, so Teresa could continue to look for special attentions paid towards herself.

The others were still worried about what Teresa might try and do to expose things.

"It's German that terrifies me. She'll be there, watching us like a gimlet," Laura said.

"She won't, she genuinely believes it was me. She may spread her nasty little tale around but I'm not sure who would listen to her." Susie also didn't care if Teresa did try to slander her as she genuinely didn't give a jot about other people's opinions. Particularly opinions based on something that wasn't even true.

Susie was quite in control of things and was very content with herself. With the midnight feast over and this latest disaster averted, it was time to complete her campaign against Mrs Ayers. Luck comes in threes, she thought, not that she needed luck.

* * *

Laura was absolutely desperate to speak with Mr Rydell. She knew that they needed to avoid being alone together more than ever but it was killing her. Teresa managed to be as slow as possible gathering up her books after German so there was no way Laura could try and linger behind.

She hoped he might leave her a note but he didn't. Tuesday came, and then Wednesday, and she was getting frantic looking out for him at lunch and around the school, hoping and hoping that they might manage to speak to one another.

The others were worried about her because she was barely eating or sleeping. In the end it was surprisingly Margery who decided they had to do something.

"He's looking even worse than you. I'm sure he thinks he's doing the right thing but I can tell he's desperate to speak to you. He's going to give the game away if he doesn't stop glancing at you all the time." It was always Margery who had noticed the way he looked at Laura, more than the others did.

"But what can I do? Teresa is always there, always the last to leave," Laura said. "And he's clearly not risking ever bumping into me alone around school any more."

"You need a chaperone," Margery said. "Charlotte and I will come up with some excuse to speak with him after class. If there's three of us then Teresa can't be so suspicious. We'll hang back in a corner and you two can have a quick chat together."

Laura hugged Margery. "You're the kindest friend ever. And I don't deserve it, given how I ditched you on both exeats."

"It's ok, I've got over it. Seeing you like this has made me realise how much it all means to you," Margery said. It had also made Margery realise that there was more to life than schoolwork. She didn't think she ever wanted to experience the desperate intensity of what Laura was going through, but at the same time she hoped she might one day get a sense of it for herself. Charlotte's relationship with Julian was so laid-back by comparison, Margery often wondered if Charlotte's heart was really in it.

But Laura and Mr Rydell: if there was such a thing as true love, perhaps this was it. As inappropriate and misguided and wrong as Margery thought it was she recognised it as more sincere than Charlotte's affair.

* * *

All went to plan. Mr Rydell was initially confused by Charlotte and Margery approaching him with some questions about German poetry translations.

But with Teresa finally gone, leaving only him and the three girls in the classroom, he realised the opportunity they were giving him.

It was still awkward talking because Charlotte and Margery would clearly be able to hear, though they tried to talk amongst themselves at the back of the room.

"How have you been?" he asked Laura. The answer was pretty obvious given how pale she was.

He also looked like he hadn't slept in weeks even though it had only been a few days since the near disaster. His hair was tousled at the front and she longed to brush it back off his face and have him kiss her, make everything okay.

"Not great. But probably no worse than you," she said.

"I'm losing sleep because of you. But we've got no other options except patience and caution."

"I know. It's so hard though. I feel like I can't even be normal around you in class, like Teresa would notice the tiniest thing," Laura said.

"We just have to get through these weeks, and look forward to the holidays." Susie had invited Laura to stay with her for the final week of the Christmas holidays. The plan was for Laura to split the time between Susie and Mr Rydell.

"I was worried you might have changed your mind about everything," she said.

"Never." He paused. "There is one thing though, it's not definite but it's probable. An old friend has offered me a job in the New Year and if they're able to replace me here I'm going to take it."

Laura was shocked, devastated. She felt like the world was collapsing around her. She stared at him, too distraught to respond.

"This makes no difference to us. If anything it's better." He tried to reassure her. "For me to stay here, it's going to be like this permanently otherwise. No more risking being with you, constantly having to suppress how I feel about you, constantly watching our backs. This way I'll be free to write to you and even phone you."

"But it won't be the same. At least here I get to see you every day." She couldn't believe he would do this to her, to them.

"Not properly though. This way we can still see each other when you're out of school. If anything we can make it more official. There are no rules, after all, about you having a relationship with someone outside school. Though we don't want to push our luck, and there are your parents to consider."

The thought of being official with him made her heart leap for a moment, but the prospect of losing him from the school was still awful. She imagined the vast, empty loneliness of the playing fields knowing that he was no longer in the groundsman's cottages. No longer anywhere there, accessible to her. No more daily glances. No more greetings when she passed him in the courtyard, knowing that he was smiling specifically at her, thinking of her.

"It will be awful without you here."

"It's awful now, being so near you and not being able to spend a second alone with you," he said. He dropped his voice. "If it wasn't for the others I would take you in my arms now. I miss holding you. You're mine, Laura, I love you and none of this changes that."

28. Risky rendezvous

Susie turned on the sugar in their next English lesson with Mr Peters. Not that he needed much encouragement. She made sure to ask him a couple of questions that flattered him to bestow his knowledge upon the class. He lapped it up.

"Why's she sucking up to that creep?" Charlotte whispered to Laura.

"No idea." They were both aware of Mr Peters' fondness for Susie and had no idea why she suddenly appeared to be reciprocating.

Susie had deliberately kept her own counsel in her affairs with Mrs Ayers and Mr Peters. She saw no need to involve the others and potentially compromise them. After all, they didn't even do Geography.

She had to stop herself laughing when she gave Mr Peters a couple of flirtatious looks and saw his reaction. He was almost beside himself. He had pursued her for so long, building her up into this unattainable object of desire, that reciprocation was overwhelming.

Not that Susie intended to ever actually reciprocate. There were certain depths to which even she, in the pursuit of victory, would not stoop.

* * *

It was break time after English, but Laura and Susie had to dash off to a rehearsal for the poetry recital. Margery and Charlotte were left on the courtyard wall, discussing plans for the Christmas holidays.

"What would your father do if he found out about your staying with Julian?" Margery asked.

"Probably explode, ground me for a thousand years and send me to a convent," Charlotte said.

"And force you to break up."

"That too. It's not like we're going to get married though. I mean I like seeing him but I can't imagine it lasting once he goes to university," Charlotte said.

Margery had been correct in her suspicion that Charlotte wasn't as into Julian as she might have been. The dalliance with the St Duncan's rugby captain was a thrill for Charlotte and a score, but more than anything it had helped her focus on what she did want and did not want for herself at that point in her life.

Charlotte liked Julian but she wasn't in love with him. If anything he represented the first in a whole world of male conquests that awaited her in future. Right now hockey was the most important thing in her life. Everything else could wait. Charlotte now knew what was out there in terms of boys but her real route to freedom would be through her own achievements.

After a lifetime of putting up with her father's rules and strictures she didn't want to get straight into the confines of another serious male relationship. She thought Julian should go on to university unencumbered, as eventually should she.

Confessing this to Margery got their friendship back on track.

"It's not that I don't like him, Margie, I really do. It's just not everything, you know?"

"Not like Laura and Mr Rydell?"

"God no. What's happening with those two terrifies me. It's all consuming, they're both practically prepared to risk their entire futures over it. I mean maybe they've both found The One and we'll all be bridesmaids in a few years, but I wouldn't want to settle for one guy forever right now, would you?" Charlotte said.

Margery didn't honestly know. She thought if it was the right person it might be quite nice. Unlike Charlotte she didn't anticipate endless future adventures for herself with a long series of exotic and exciting men. In fact Margery thought it would be less of a distraction to meet the right person early on, as Laura perhaps had. With that achieved and settled, one could then concentrate on other things. Certainly Laura was topping English by a mile now, despite Mr Peters' amorous yearnings towards Susie and subsequently generous marking of her work.

* * *

Lunch was particularly revolting that day: something described as curry that appeared to consist of fat and gristle in an oily, orange-brown sauce. As usual Charlotte wolfed everything down barely noticing what it was, but even Margery baulked at today's fare.

For Laura it was egg-day again. As Charlotte had warned her, the vegetarian options basically alternated hard boiled eggs with grated cheddar. Laura had been sick of both long before half-term, but not enough to rescind her new diet and return to the threat of liver.

"I bet you can't wait until the holidays and actually eating some steak and chicken," Charlotte said.

"And bacon," Laura said. School bacon was awful, flabby and undercooked, but at least it tasted of something.

With a hiatus on her affair with Mr Rydell, at least in terms of the physical side, she had thrown herself into her work. Most of her energy went into the subjects she liked, particularly History and English.

They were being kept so busy with all the rehearsals for the various end of term activities that it helped distract her from wanting to look out for him all the time. The school was a whirl of preparations for the Sixth Form play with St Duncan's, the carol service, the poetry recital plus end of term exams and the house hockey cup.

Michaelmas House had high hopes of victory. They had several school squad members in house but most of all they had Charlotte Bevan, now pretty much the star player of Francis Hall despite still being in the Lower School. "Amazing to see progress like that," Miss Partridge remarked to Miss Vine. "The natural talent has always been there, but it's the focus and enthusiasm that has brought it all together." She was planning on approaching Charlotte's parents about national junior trials.

"Do you want to play in the Junior house team?" Charlotte asked Laura. She herself was captain that year.

"We'll win, won't we, with you on the side?" The house tournament was always divided between the Lower and the Upper school, so Charlotte wouldn't be playing on the Sixth Form team despite her ability.

"We'd better not lose. There are some keen fourth formers but there's still a place for you if you want it," Charlotte said.

"Is Teresa Hubert playing?"

"No, she should be, but she was so pissed off about me getting into the Firsts that I think she's turned her back on it all entirely. I even heard her ask Miss Vine if she could switch to cross-country next term."

Next term. When Mr Rydell probably wouldn't be there any longer. It was horrifying to think of, the school would be empty for her without him. Laura needed to distract herself. "I'll play then, if you need me."

* * *

Susie hit pay dirt when Mr Peters handed their English exercise books back after marking their latest essays.

Tucked inside hers, on personalised lavender notepaper that reeked of his cologne, was an invitation. "Come to my flat at 5pm today. Urgent." Mr Peters had signed it with his initials in his usual florid hand.

It opened up a world of possibilities. But there was one that Susie easily fixed upon.

Finding a pen with ink that matched as closely as possible, Susie took an envelope and copied the Head of English's capital P to write "Pat" on it. It looked convincingly like his writing. She slipped the note inside and sealed it. Then she grabbed Mary Rudge who was passing by.

"Can you do me a huge favour and drop this in Mrs Ayers' pigeonhole by the staff room? Thanks a million!"

Mary was happy to oblige since she was going near that way anyway. Susie felt content. The chips were cast: in good time she would see how they would fall.

* * *

Lessons had finished for the day and it was games again: hockey for Charlotte and Susie, and cross country for Laura and Margery. They set off together but Margery was much slower than usual due to a sore ankle. They ended up right at the back but in the end Margery decided she couldn't even jog.

So they walked along falling further and further behind everyone else, Margery hobbling uncomfortably. Eventually Miss Vine caught up with them on her bicycle - not fit enough herself to run, she cycled around the pitches to keep an eye on the runners - and asked what was wrong.

"Something with my ankle," Margery said.

"We'd better get you to the school nurse."

"I can take her," Laura offered.

"No that's fine, you run along and catch up with the others." If truth be told Miss Vine was as glad of the excuse to escape the cold and windy pitches as any of them. She left with Margery limping along, and Laura resumed a gentle jog. It was nice being by herself, she didn't particularly want to catch up with the others.

As the path took her past the wasteland area, which was a hedge and some bushes that sloped down to the brook, she heard her name called. It was Mr Rydell.

"The coast is clear, come and join me."

She pushed through a gap in the hedge after checking no one was observing her. "What are you doing here?" She was thrilled and bewildered to see him.

"I saw you coming from a distance, and Margery leave with Miss Vine. I wanted to see you." He had her in his arms within seconds and they were kissing passionately, desperately.

She broke off. "We'll get caught."

"Not here we won't, it's completely concealed." He was right. She looked around and saw that the shrubbery and the angle of the bank screened them completely from any sight of the school grounds.

"They'll notice I'm gone though."

He silenced her with another kiss and she let him crush her against his body as she breathed in his scent and his warmth, longing for his heat all the more in the chill of the air.

There was a tree trunk with ivy growing up it and he turned her and pushed her against it, facing away from him.

"What are you doing?"

"I need you, Laura. I've missed you like hell these past couple of weeks."

"We can't, not here..." she broke off as he slid his hands beneath her underwear, roughly tugging her tracksuit down. One finger slid between her legs and he started playing with her clit. She gasped and held onto the tree, her fingers twining in the thick ivy.

His fingers were firm, forceful. He was getting her so wet that she couldn't resist, that she would take him inside her here, in the open air, despite all the risk and everything they had been through.

Helpless, her face pressed against the bark and leaves, she felt him grasp her hips and angle them towards his hardness.

"Oh god we can't..." she made a last attempt to move away from him but he was unyielding. He gripped her firmly and pulled her towards him.

"I need this Laura. And so do you."

He was as hard as a rock. It made him easy for him to slide inside her despite the unusual angle and her initial resistance. She did want him - as much as he wanted her. It felt amazing as he entered her, she could feel every inch of his hardness, deep, deep inside her.

"We fit so well." He groaned as he spoke, pulling back and then thrusting hard into her, pushing her against the tree. Unyielding, it allowed him to slam into her with force, as hard as he wanted, as long as he wanted.

She was a mass of raw sensation: the roughness of the tree, her body forced against it, the cold air, the wonderful huge hardness that he was possessing her with. All her nerves were on edge on fire. She didn't even care if Jenkins showed up with Mrs Grayson, though she tried not to cry out too much.

She wanted him to touch her clit again and she tried to change the angle to get pressure there but he denied her.

"No, you're going to come from this alone. Me inside you." Once again he was commanding her, driving her closer to the edge.

She couldn't use her own hands because he was pinning them with own.

"Please touch me," she begged him. She was being pushed against the bark but she wanted his actual hands on her. He refused her. He wanted to bring her to the edge solely with his hardness inside her.

"I don't care how long it takes, I can do this to you for a very long time, but you are going to come for me like this," he ordered.

She had no choice but to take it.

Then at some point the sensations in her shifted, and she felt waves begin in her stomach. It was a different kind of release than he normally gave her, it built more slowly and it made her feel even more dizzy. It was the relentlessness of him pushing inside her, giving her in no respite, owning her core.

Surprising herself she began to climax and couldn't stop crying out, and he put his hand in front of her mouth which only made the physical sensations elsewhere in her body even more intense. The more she struggled the deeper and harder he was within her.

She came like she had never come before. Intensely, bucking against him, almost sobbing. She felt him make extra thrusts at the same time, and then the sensation of his hot essence released in her.

She was laughing now, so overwhelmed, so exhausted. Overjoyed.

"That was good for you?" he asked.

"Unbelievably."

"We are perfect together," he said. He refastened his clothing, and pull her down to the ground, putting his are around her. "At times like this I feel like just leaving and taking you with me."

"Are you still leaving?" She had become resigned to the fact now the shock of the idea was past.

"I have no choice. Look at us. Look at me. This is out of control." His hand traced the side of her face. "I want to be able to be with you, to communicate with you more openly. I know we'll have to disguise letters and calls for a while but at least you won't be at risk of expulsion if I no longer work here."

29. Entrapment

"Quick, we need to get to the music lawn." Susie hurried the others after they had finished changing out of their games kit. "Not a moment to lose."

The music lawn ran between the music building and the section of the main school which contained the Maths classrooms and two flats occupied by Mr Peters and Mr Tyrrell. From the wooden bench by the music room door they looked directly onto it.

"What's going on?" The others were bewildered by the urgency.

"Sssh. Just sit back and watch," Susie said.

"It's freezing and we have to get to early prep," Margery complained.

"We've got twenty minutes. Just wait."

From their vantage point they saw Mrs Ayers striding into the main doorway, and taking the stairs that led to the flats. She looked even angrier than usual.

Seconds later they heard a shriek and raised voices.

"Pure Shakespeare," Susie said. "True love never did run smooth."

* * *

Mrs Ayers had been more irritated than intrigued to received Mr Peters' unexpected note. Its presumptive and commanding tone, providing no reason for his summons, irked her. She didn't care for Mr Peters at the best of times, she thought he was an old fool. They had clashed on more than one occasion.

The note was also inconvenient as Mrs Ayers was busy that afternoon. She had had a very difficult morning with annoying things happening to her again in the classroom. She was certain they were pranks, but there was a subtlety about them that left room for doubt. While she suspected Susie Clarke she still had no proof.

So she strode off to Mr Peters' flat in a particularly foul mood.

Already fired up and ready to give him a piece of her mind if he had led her on a wild goose chase, she knocked on his door.

"Come in!" he called.

Mrs Ayers opened the door and stood inside Mr Peters' sitting room, her face set in its typically grim line.

Nothing could prepare her for what awaited.

There - at the bedroom door - clad in a black silk dressing gown with a glass of champagne in each hand, appeared the Head of English. The gown revealed an expanse of greying chest hair and his lips held a lecherous leer.

The smile died on his face when he saw Mrs Ayers. He paled as she shrieked and went crimson with outrage.

"What the fuck are you doing here?" Forgetting himself in his shock, Mr Peters swore. "Where's Susanna?"

"I beg your pardon!" No one had ever managed to imbue these words with such fury and disgust as Mrs Ayers did at that moment. "I am here because of your note."

"I never sent you any bloody note. Oh Christ!" The realisation was dawning. How on earth had this monstrous woman intercepted his message to Susie Clarke? "What the hell have you done with her? I suppose you gave her another detention you vicious old boot."

Mrs Ayers started screeching at him for this and Mr Peters gave back as good as he got. He was enraged with disappointment that the hag had wrecked his romantic rendezvous.

At some point during the row his silk robe slipped open. He wore nothing beneath it.

Below his paunch the remnants of his ardour for the anticipated encounter with Susie were only too clear.

Mrs Ayers got it into her head that he was about to sexually assault her, started screaming even more loudly and fled as Mr Peters fumbled to close his gown again while trying not to spill champagne everywhere.

* * *

Outside the four girls couldn't make out what was being said but they could hear the volume of the row. Susie was doubled over nearly weeping with laughter.

The next thing they saw was Mrs Ayers come clattering out of the doorway, striding off in the direction of the staff room practically at a trot.

"And the bad fairy flees the feast," said Susie.

She explained to the others what had happened with the note. "If only we could have actually been there to see his face. And hers."

"Imagine if he opened the door to her naked," Charlotte said. "Perhaps that's why she was screaming."

It was not a pleasant image.

"I wonder what will happen," Laura said. "I suppose he couldn't really tell her the note was meant for you. But what will he say to you next time he sees you? Will he know you deliberately sent it to her?"

"I really don't know. If he asks, I'll say she confiscated it from me. Or that somebody took it from me and gave it to her." Susie wasn't worried about what would happen next. Instead she was enjoying the chaos as for once, in terms of school rules at least, she was totally innocent.

* * *

"It's him or me, I won't put up with it any longer." Mrs Ayers was screeching at the Headmistress after her traumatic encounter with Mr Peters. Her face was crimson and her eyes wild.

Mrs Grayson did her best to calm the Geography teacher down but she appeared to be having some kind of breakdown.

It had been difficult to establish exactly what had happened, other than Mr Peters allegedly having made an untoward approach to Mrs Ayers. In reality the Headmistress found it very hard to believe he would attempt such a thing.

But every time she tried to get the facts calmly from Mrs Ayers, the latter started shrieking about "disgusting perverts" and losing her temper even more.

"I will not stay in this school for as long as that... that deviant remains among us."

It was clear that the Headmistress would need to speak with Mr Peters to try and sort the matter out.

* * *

The Head of English was still at a loss to know how his invitation to Susie had found its way into Mrs Ayers' possession. He had by now had time to recover from his own shock and rehearse his own convincing version of events.

The problem was the note. He didn't know where it was or if Mrs Ayers still had it. Were it found, he would have to come up with an explanation of whom it had really been written to. Claiming it was a forged practical joke would be difficult, given that it was composed on his personal notepaper.

Clearly he couldn't admit it to it have been intended for Susie or any other pupil. His thoughts went to Miss Wingrove. Much as he detested her, she might be useful to his purposes now. And there was no need for her to be any the wiser.

"A dreadful and embarrassing misunderstanding," he told Mrs Grayson. "I had of course intended the invitation for quite a different member of staff. I'm sure I needn't put her in a compromising position by naming names. How it came to be in dear Mrs Ayers' possession I really can't say."

"Mrs Ayers claims you were in a state of undress and began verbally abusing her," the Headmistress told him.

"Not at all. If I perhaps spoke strongly it was due to my own embarrassment, and I no doubt raised my own voice to try and calm her."

Mrs Grayson knew both characters well enough to be quite certain there had been a blazing and vicious row on both sides. She wondered whom the note had really been intended for.

She hoped it wasn't written to one of the Sixth Form girls but given Mr Peters' proclivities this remained possible.

She wished she could sack the pair of them. If only they didn't get such exceptional Oxbridge results.

* * *

Susie was on a high all night. She couldn't know what exactly had happened - or what was still happening - but she felt in her bones it was something good.

"Mr Peters might be mad if he finds out you gave his note to her," Charlotte said.

"I'll just say I never got it. Or that I left my English books in the Geography room by accident. He'll so desperately want to believe it was all a big misunderstanding that he'll lap up whatever I tell him." Susie was confident in her influence where the Head of English was concerned.

"What about next term though?" Laura asked. "Won't it be a bit of a bore having him constantly making his approaches?"

"He'll give up sooner or later. Besides, won't there be another school play next term? He'll be busy with the Sixth Form girls for that."

They were supposed to be getting an early night in preparation for the House hockey tournament tomorrow but no one felt like sleep. Excitement always grew as the end of term approached, and Susie had increased the fever beyond measure.

30. Fallout

It was freezing showing up to the hockey pitch in the regulation games skirt and sweater. How Charlotte did it in blithe spirit every Saturday was inexplicable. They were allowed to wear tracksuits for regular practice but on match days the official kit was required.

"I can't understand how they endlessly punish us for hemlines a millimetre above the knee then expect us to wear these micro skirts for hockey," Laura said.

The games skirts, in the school colour of maroon, were teamed with matching gym knickers. "Granny-pants" that nearly reached the navel and were reviled by everyone.

"If Mr Rydell could only see you now!" Susie said to Laura as they got ready in the changing room. Susie had also agreed to play. Like Laura she was a competent player when she applied herself, which was rarely.

Laura was already nervous about the prospect of Mr Rydell watching. She wanted him to be there, but no one looked their best splattered with mud, out of breath and with the winter wind reddening their nose.

The news had spread rapidly around the school that Mr Peters and Mrs Ayers had declared open warfare. Speculation was rife as to what had occurred, but Susie managed to circulate a rumour that Mrs Ayers had made advances to Mr

Peters and been rejected. It did not take long for this to become the dominant theory, even reaching staffroom ears.

This gossip overtook the usual excitement over the House hockey tournament. Last year Michaelmas had narrowly won against Whitsun. This time Charlotte planned to smash them. But instead of speculation over this year's winner the main topic of conversation was the shenanigans in the staff room.

Everyone was dying to see if both teachers would appear at the match so they could witness the frosty air and hopefully a further row. But they were to be disappointed, as Mr Peters stayed away.

Mr Rydell was among the staff members who did turn out to watch. Laura had to walk right past him. She briefly caught his eye and he looked her up and down. His gaze was both amused and appreciative. She flushed and could feel his eyes burning into her back as she went onto the pitch.

"Someone obviously approves of your hemline," Susie whispered to her.

It irked Laura that she had to pretend in public as though she and Mr Rydell were essentially strangers. Before it had been a thrill, a secret joke between them. Now she was getting tired of the endless discretion.

She looked at him talking with Miss Wingrove and smiling at something the English teacher said, and for a moment Laura hated her. How was she allowed to so freely chat and laugh with him, when she didn't know him a fraction as intimately as Laura did?

The whistle blew and she threw herself into the game. It was against Lammas and they easily won. To no one's surprise, Michaelmas and Whitsun both ended up in the final again. Whitsun had also won their early matches with ease.

It was a bitterly fought game. Even with Charlotte leading the side it was no quick victory. In the first half Whitsun scored twice with Michaelmas only managing a single goal, all early on.

At half time while they sucked orange segments Susie caught sight of Mrs Ayers glowering from the sidelines. Susie determined not to give her any satisfaction that day. She needed to keep the momentum going. It wasn't enough to win: Michaelmas needed to vanquish Whitsun.

Finally putting some effort into her game, she surprised everyone with a rare streak of brilliance. Charlotte, always a generous player, saw Susie putting on a spurt and set her up for several goals. Susie's scoring spree in the second half brought them to 2:6 in favour of Michaelmas. It was an extraordinary turnaround.

Susie's triumph was more than salt in the wounded pride of Mrs Ayers. It was boiling acid.

* * *

The humiliation of her House on the pitch, in no small part due to Susie Clarke, did nothing to distract Mrs Ayers from her rage over Mr Peters. Instead the two became conflated in her mind. She also remembered, though without realising the significance, his reference to Susie earlier in their row. He had dared to criticise her discipline of the girl!

Clearly the brat had wound Mr Peters around her finger along with the other staff who had had words with Mrs Ayers over the past weeks. The Headmistress had not been the only person who questioned the endless detentions she had given Susie. A couple of other staff members had also raised eyebrows.

Mrs Ayers felt besieged. She felt that the entire school was persecuting her. And it was all the Clarke girl's fault. She wanted only two things: Susie gone and Mr Peters gone. She knew the former would be more difficult to achieve since the girl was so sly and manipulative. But it had become an all-consuming obsession.

* * *

"What a day. What a glorious, glorious day."

The four of them sat in the courtyard that evening basking in their victory. It was worth the exhaustion.

"I honestly think I feel better about today than the first time I played for the school eleven," Charlotte said.

Their contentment was short-lived as the shadow of Mrs Ayers fell upon them. "Susie Clarke and Charlotte Bevan, your socks are down. A demerit point each!"

"Oh for god's sake, it's Saturday night," Susie said.

"A detention for answering back and swearing!" Mrs Ayers shrieked.

Susie looked at her. She assessed the situation. Now, she felt, was the time to strike.

"No thanks."

Mrs Ayers was momentarily confounded. "You'll take a detention," she repeated.

"No, I won't this time, thanks all the same," said Susie. Her tone was pointedly flippant. The others sat there, hardly daring to breathe.

No one had ever actually refused a detention before. Mrs Ayers had experienced acquiescence, sullenness, apathy, pleading, profuse apologising but never this.

"It's not up to you to accept or not. You'll be in detention this week and the week after for insolence."

"I'm afraid I won't. I've had quite enough detentions from you." Susie's polite smile and the contempt she put into her words incensed the Geography teacher beyond measure. Already unbalanced through her hatred of the schoolgirl and her recent traumatic ordeal with Mr Peters, she started screeching at Susie. A slew of insults flew from her lips. Other people around them were turning to watch.

Susie merely sat there, smiling while refusing to respond, goading Mrs Ayers even further. Eventually she lunged at the girl, grabbing her by her shoulders and starting to shake her while she shouted and.ranted at her.

Laura and Charlotte, on either side of Susie, tried to intervene and get Susie away. But Mrs Ayers was deranged by her fury. As Susie struggled in Mrs Ayers' grasp, Miss Partridge and Miss Vine appeared and rushed over to find out what was going on.

Seeing Mrs Ayers assaulting Susie, Miss Partridge managed to drag them apart and ordered the girls away. "All of you, back to your House or supper or wherever you should be." They left in a mix of relief and excitement.

"Pat, what the hell got into you? We'll have to go to the Head, half the school has seen anyway." The Games mistress managed to get the Geography teacher out of the courtyard and towards the staffroom, Miss Vine following.

* * *

"She disliked me and became increasingly vindictive," was Susie's explanation to the Headmistress the next morning. She had a scratch and bruise on the side of her face and had tied her hair back deliberately to expose them. There were also marks on her arms from where the Geography teacher had grasped her.

Mrs Grayson had thought it better for the matter to rest overnight as far as the girls were concerned. She had already ordered Mrs Ayers onto immediate sick leave.

"Did you give her any cause?" Mrs Grayson asked. She knew that however Susie may have provoked the Geography teacher nothing warranted a physical attack. Susie would also be perfectly within her rights to tell her parents and make a formal complaint. But the housemistress felt by instinct that Susie would not do this.

She looked at the girl. Susie's expression wore its usual mask of polite composure. Yet in her eyes there was a light of both satisfaction and defiance. Susie had gone into battle, and she had won.

Either way Mrs Grayson had to get to the bottom of this. She already regretted not paying more heed when Grace Grant had raised concerns with her several weeks earlier.

Susie had no intention of admitting anything. "You have seen my work," Susie replied. She had brought her immaculate Geography exercise book with her.

"This is about more than work, isn't it?"

Susie paused. She was thinking past the Headmistress's question which didn't really need a response since they both knew what the answer was. "She had a choice," Susie said.

"Yes, she did. But so did you."

Susie couldn't feel any remorse for goading the Geography teacher past the point of no return. "She was a blight," she said, using Charlotte's phrase.

Mrs Grayson felt partly culpable in the matter. Pat Ayers had been a problem for years and really something should have been done before now to moderate some of the worst excesses of her character. Perhaps her breakdown was inevitable.

But there was no doubt that Susie Clarke had knowingly and deliberately accelerated it.

"We all have a choice, Susie, even if we have no obligation, when it comes to compassion and forbearance."

Susie felt momentarily small at these words. But she had never regarded her task as noble, only necessary. And it was done.

31. The catalyst

Mrs Grayson, Miss Wingrove and Grace Grant were discussing the situation.

"The problem is that she didn't actually do anything," Mrs Grayson said, referring to Susie. "Not something that one could pin down so to speak."

There was less to say about Mrs Ayers. Her breakdown had been of little surprise to many of her colleagues who had regarded her as unstable for years. Miss Partridge, who had a degree in Geography, was taking her classes until the end of term. There was no regret, only relief, among the girls that she was gone. And among the staff too, not least of all Mr Peters who regarded her exit as a personal victory.

"She's more of a catalyst," Miss Wingrove said. "She doesn't necessarily do anything herself, but others seem to behave differently around her. She's a nice girl though, bright and popular. Loyal to her friends," she added, thinking of a couple of times where Susie had covered for someone else's late arrival or provided a similar favour.

"She clearly has little respect for authority," Mrs Grayson said.

Grace Grant had been privately troubled ever since Susie's odd confession about visiting Mr Rydell, even though he had corroborated her story. The whole thing had made little sense then and her unease had only grown. Miss Wingrove's words began to cast a new light on things.

The housemistress hadn't really considered why Susie might lie, except for self-aggrandisement or to create drama. Schoolgirls did this so often that fantastic tales were par for the course.

But what if Susie had lied to protect someone else?

Most likely it would be one of her closest friends, her three dorm mates. Not Margery, certainly, and Charlotte seemed highly improbable. She was so focused on her hockey these days. Which left Laura. Could she have visited Mr Rydell that night?

Grace Grant thought about Laura that term. So far as she knew the girl was still doing well at her lessons, was healthy, maintained her friendships. It was a time of change for many girls, growing into womanhood.

Was it possible that Laura was the one who had propositioned Mr Rydell, with Susie lying to save her from embarrassment?

But if that was the case, why had he backed Susie's story? She couldn't disregard his own statements, unless...

Unless something very different and very, very troubling was happening.

"You're pensive, Grace, anything to add?" Mrs Grayson asked her. "I must say these are all complications we don't need at this stage of the school year. It's bad enough having to find a replacement Geography teacher mid-year, but now German as well."

"German?" Grace Grant was startled.

"Yes. That new young man has got another job offer. I can't say it surprises me and perhaps to some extent it's a relief," the Headmistress said. It was always a risk, hiring a young male teacher among adolescent girls, and they all knew it.

"Nothing has happened, though?" Grace Grant asked.

"There has been some minor silliness. We had several Sixth Form girls suddenly wanting to switch to A-level German in the first couple of weeks which of course couldn't be accommodated. And the usual things like love poems fluttering out of his pigeonhole. Though he's dealt with it all very well and has the respect of the girls, not simply their admiration."

But perhaps there had been more than "silliness", Grace Grant thought. She needed more time to think about this.

* * *

Miss Wingrove was heartily glad that the poetry recital was a school event only without parents invited to watch. This had been considered but was ruled out due to time and logistical constraints.

Susie Clarke's rendition of "The Flea" was definitely not something an audience of mothers and fathers needed to hear. Even without Mr Peters' special coaching it was enough to make the Earl of Rochester blush. Miss Wingrove couldn't even bring herself to look at Mr Peters' face during Susie's performance. Surely even John Donne hadn't intended quite that amount of innuendo in his lines?

But it was Laura who took her breath away. Laura had originally been practising something by Keats but had changed her mind at the last moment. She claimed it was because Teresa Hubert was also reciting Keats, but several other poets had been chosen by multiple girls.

Instead, Laura read Shelley. She displayed none of the self-consciousness or nerves of many of the other reciters. She merely stood in the centre of the stage, her gaze fixed above and beyond the audience, making no apparent effort to connect with them. Her voice was still and calm.

"See the mountains kiss high heaven,

"And the waves clasp one another"

Miss Wingrove had never thought of the poem as particularly sorrowful before, but spoken by Laura it was unbearably sad.

"And the sunlight clasps the earth,

"And the moonbeams kiss the sea -

"What is all this sweet work worth

"If thou kiss not me?"

Sitting at the back of the hall with the rest of the staff, Grace Grant now felt she knew all she needed to know. Laura of a term ago would never have managed to speak these lines in the way she did now. Grace Grant did not have a background in literature and knew nothing of the context of the poem. But the poignancy, the desolation, the sensuality conveyed were those of a young woman, not a girl.

She didn't need to look at Mr Rydell - though she did look - to know that his gaze would be transfixed on Laura. The admiration in his eyes, the hunger. Everyone else was watching the stage so Grace Grant was the only one who saw how captivated he was by her. How far had this gone, the housemistress wondered. And how had it happened with no one knowing?

Despite this he was leaving the school. Or perhaps because of it.

* * *

Grace Grant had no concrete proof but nor did she want any because it might force her hand. She did however feel a duty towards Laura as her housemistress.

She summoned Laura to her office with the invitation for a "chat and a cup of tea".

"What does Gi-Gi want with you?" Charlotte asked.

"I have no idea. She sounded quite nice so I don't think I'm in trouble." Laura hoped she wasn't in trouble. She couldn't see why she would be.

"She might be digging about something else," Susie said.

Laura vowed to keep her lips sealed regarding anything that might compromise them, from the midnight feast to Susie's redirection of Mr Peters' note.

"I know you won't say anything, but she might try to catch you out." Susie had been wary of the housemistress since her own interview about Mr Rydell.

Laura knocked and entered the housemistress's office at the appointed time. She had always really liked the room. It was a calm place.

Grace Grant ushered her to one of the arm chairs by the window. It was where she held her informal, pastoral chats. Her desk was for more serious business.

Sinking onto the green velvet cushions, Laura waited for Miss Grant to speak.

"It's always a long term, the Autumn term," Grace Grant began. "I expect we're all looking forward to the holidays."

It was the equivalent to commenting on the weather, Laura thought. Whatever the housemistress wanted to say was clearly a difficult topic to broach. She took a sip of the tea that she had been given.

"You've all had quite a lot of excitement this term with some of the St Duncan's boys, I believe," Miss Grant said.

This was an odd one. Particularly as Laura hadn't really had any excitement with them at all.

"I know it must be quite exciting seeing older boys, but they do eventually go off to university where there are quite a lot of other distractions."

"Yes, these things don't always last," Laura said, thinking of Charlotte and Julian and wondering why Miss Grant was saying all this to her.

"I know it's all very thrilling when someone older than you shows interest. But letting such a relationship influence your life choices now may be something you regret in future," the housemistress said to her. Her eyes were kind but concerned.

At some point Laura realised that Grace Grant wasn't talking about the St Duncan's boys at all.

"You girls all have so many exciting years ahead of you. It would be an enormous shame to limit your options too early," Miss Grant said.

Laura didn't know how Miss Grant had found out. But she realised that the housemistress somehow knew about her and Mr Rydell and was worried for Laura's sake. Grace Grant saw that Laura also understood what she was really talking about.

"You also have to consider whether the older person is really being fair as well, to put you in such a position," she continued.

"Do you mean like Lucy Martin? I don't plan for something like that to happen to me," Laura said.

"I've always regretted what happened to Lucy," Miss Grant said. "I wish we could have done something more for her. I wish I had been able to prevent her from getting into her situation in the first place. But when something like that happens, a bridge is crossed."

She put down her teacup.

"What do you do with your life outside school is up to you, Laura. Soon you will all be adults and able to make your own choices about everything. But you are such a talented girl with so much promise. It would be very disappointing if you were distracted from realising your potential." Grace Grant looked at her directly, serious and also sad.

"Love is a wonderful thing but it doesn't always last. You have to think about what you owe to yourself. Don't close doors when you can leave them open."

32. Farewell

It was the last day of term. There were no lessons that afternoon just packing, clearing up, and getting ready to go home for the holidays.

The four of them were sitting on a bench outside Michaelmas House when Mr Rydell walked past. "Come for a walk with me?" he said to Laura.

She went with him. It was his last ever day at the school and it was too late for either of them to get in trouble for a simple walk. She didn't care what people thought, or that Teresa Hubert was nearby.

There were many raised eyebrows, not least Teresa's.

"Why is Laura walking with Mr Rydell?" she asked the other three. Her tone was accusing.

Susie shrugged. "They've become friends through their shared passion for German."

Teresa was enraged by her flippancy. "It was her I saw that night, wasn't it? It wasn't you at all. You lied."

"I have no idea what you think you saw."

"Is she having an affair with him? It's absolutely disgusting, he's her teacher. He should be sacked."

"Given it's his last day today, it won't be much of a sacking, will it?" Susie gave an infuriating smile. Next to her Charlotte and Margery were also enjoying Teresa's fury. They had won every battle against Teresa's faction this term and this was the cherry on the cake.

"She'll still be in trouble though, when Mrs Grayson finds out."

"Finds out what?" Charlotte asked.

"You know exactly what." Teresa was getting furious at the three of them, sitting there smugly and trying to brush her off.

"Why don't you go to Grace Grant with your concerns?" Susie said. Laura had told them about her talk with the housemistress. Grace Grant had clearly made a decision not to act even though she knew that something had happened and Susie doubted Teresa's tattle-tales would influence her.

"I could go straight to Mrs Grayson." They all knew she wouldn't. All things said and done, Teresa was a coward.

"If you feel it's serious enough and you have the evidence to support your accusations, then by all means do so." Susie turned from Teresa to signal that the conversation was over, and their enraged but defeated enemy had no choice but to return to her own affairs.

* * *

"I will miss you," he said.

It was a grey December day with a leaden sky, a horrible day for saying goodbyes.

"Miss Grant knows." Seeing him start in shock, Laura hurried to reassure him. "It's ok, she isn't going to say anything. She just made it clear that she knows - I'm not sure how - and gave me some pointed advice about boyfriends and being careful not to ruin my life."

"I hope I'm not ruining your life."

"You have transformed it," she told him.

"For better or worse?"

"Better beyond anything." But she knew that being with him had made things better but harder too. She couldn't shut the door on what she knew now and what she had experienced. It had set her apart from the others, from her peers.

From her parents too, since there was no way she could tell them about him.

They had reached the place where the path ran past the wasteland area. He turned to her.

"Be careful next term. They never found that vagrant, did they?"

"There was no vagrant to find."

Now he was leaving she figured it was fine to tell him. They both owed Susie so much anyway. She explained about the midnight feast and the close call with Jenkins.

She had been uncertain as to how he might react, but he laughed. "That girl, she's unbelievable," he said. "I would be worried about her leading you astray, except I've already done that."

"I chose, you didn't lead me," Laura said.

There was a lot to be grateful for when it came to Susie. She had extended endless invitations to Laura to come and stay with her, all with facilitating her relationship with Mr Rydell in mind. Laura might even be going to see her in Italy for a week in January.

She looked up at the black boughs of the copper beeches silhouetted against the winter sky. Would it be warmer in Italy?

Just a couple of months ago she had sat under these trees with her friends, still warm in the September sun, innocent of everything she knew now.

She looked at him. The angle of his jaw, the dark hair, his strength. She knew that he was what she wanted and she couldn't ever imagine a time when he wouldn't be.

"I could probably kiss you here, right in the open air, and get away with it," he said.

For a wild moment Laura wanted him to kiss her, to declare their feelings openly in front of anyone who might be watching. But the thought of Grace Grant held her back. She had offered unprecedented discretion to Laura, even though she must have felt an obligation to report what she suspected. Out of respect to her, Laura could not be public with him.

"It's enough that I've gone for a walk with you, that will raise enough eyebrows," she said.

"Will you get into trouble for it?" He looked concerned.

"No, just some remarks I expect." Laura wasn't too worried. Susie and Charlotte would deal with Teresa for her.

They were walking the full circuit of the fields, which would eventually bring them back to Michaelmas House. Every step was a step closer to goodbye. At least for now. She wished she could slow time.

"So I'll see you in Italy then?" he said.

It sounded so far away in distance and in time. He read her thoughts. "It's only three weeks away."

"It still seems forever though, compared to seeing you every day here."

"Let's go this way." He took her on a brief diversion around to where the pavilion was, instead of straight back to Michaelmas House.

"This will really get tongues wagging."

"What they don't see they can't know," he said, leading he around the back where they were out of eyesight. Laura felt a slight shudder looking at the now-repaired window. "The scene of the crime?" he asked.

"Something like that."

"It's also where I first touched your hand. And I knew that I wasn't imagining what was between us."

"And what was that?" she asked, smiling.

His lips answered her. They were warm and firm on hers in the chilly air. She savoured the feel of him, the taste, the intimacy of his tongue entwining with hers. Felt how tall he was as he had to bend down to kiss her as she reached up to meet him. Felt the strength of his arms around her. The power, both physical and emotional, he had over her.

"That I love you," he said, as he broke away. He fingered her necklace, the one had had given her. "And that I hope this will be on a ring one day."

She kissed him again. "I love you too."

Just three weeks. Somehow she would endure it.

* * *

Laura brazened it out when she got back to Michaelmas House. She told anyone who asked that she had been discussing Goethe with Mr Rydell. She at least had a reputation for being good at literature and poetry, so some were convinced and silenced.

Susie beat the remainder into submission by accusing them of having jealous crushes of their own. "My Rydell, you're my idol!" she chanted at one girl.

Teresa knew what she knew and was all the more enraged that Laura and Susie appeared to be getting away with everything again. But people were already trickling away, more interested in going home and seeing their families again than school gossip. By January it would be long forgotten.

Susie was the first of the four to go, her parents driving up in a grey Bentley. Her mother looked very glamorous from what they could see through the window. "Easy to see where Susie gets it from," Charlotte said.

So the three of them sat together once more.

"It feels like another lifetime, when I think back to the start of this term," Laura said. "I know it's the longest term but it feels like years have passed."

As devastated as she was by Mr Rydell leaving, she was relieved the intensity of the term was over. They all needed a break.

"I wonder if The Axe will be back next term?" Charlotte asked.

"I don't think so. I don't think you could come back after that," Margery said. She had mixed feelings about what Susie had done. All in all it was for the best, but Mrs Ayers' public breakdown had made her uneasy.

"So it's off to Italy for you?" Charlotte said to Laura. She herself was looking forward to seeing Julian, there would be a couple of balls around Christmas and she was going to try and find a date for Margery.

"Yes, I can't wait. Skiing too, if the snows come."

And him. Her future. Her soulmate. The man who had taught her more than she could have ever imagined. Lessons she would remember long after Latin verbs and calculus had faded from memory. Forbidden lessons: lessons of desire, lessons of love.

Glossary of terms

Some of the British English terms used in *Forbidden Lessons* may be unfamiliar to non UK readers. This glossary is provided as a guide.

A-levels

Final high school exams, usually only three to four subjects are studied, in the last two years

Common room

Room used for leisure or social activities by pupils

Demerit

Penalty point imposed for a wrongdoing

Dorm

(Dormitory) bedroom for multiple pupils at a boarding school

Exeat

A kind of short school holiday, when boarding pupils are allowed to leave the school overnight

Games

Term used for sport, physical exercise

Gated

Gonfined to school grounds, similar to grounding

Half-term

A short holiday half-way through a school term

House

Schools are often divided into houses, usually for the purposes of residential accommodation

Mufti

Regular clothes, being out of school uniform

Out of bounds

An area on or off school grounds to which access is forbidden

Oxbridge

Oxford + Cambridge, England's two most elite universities, similar to Ivy League

Prep

(Preparation) a term used for homework, and the time allotted to complete homework

Sixth form

The final two years of school, when one is studying for A-levels

About Noël Cades

Noël Cades is a British writer who currently lives in Sydney, Australia. A fan of romance from historic to erotic, some of Noël's favourite authors include Jilly Cooper, Jackie Collins, Elizabeth Rolls and Victoria Holt.

You can contact Noël at noel@noelcades.com

Noël's website is at http://www.noelcades.com

www.ingramcontent.com/pod-product-compliance
Lightning Source LLC
Chambersburg PA
CBHW030514020726
47494CB00004B/1097